"GOT SOME BAD news," Annie said, her voice sounding about as serious as it could be. "It didn't take Fleet and his crew more than a few hours to track over three hundred missing women who matched the profile of the women in the mine. He ran the search from two years before you found the women to now."

Lott felt his stomach twist into a tight knot. "Three hundred?"

Julia's eyes across the table grew wide in a look of horror.

"How wide an area did he search?" Lott asked.

"All of Montana, Colorado, New Mexico and every state west," Annie said.

"All basically a two day drive from the Las Vegas area," Lott said.

"Pretty much," Annie said. "Not all of these women who are missing will be involved, of course. But if our killer did eleven women a year for the last fifteen years, that's over a hundred and fifty women."

Lott had no idea what to say to that.

Nothing at all.

Finally Julia asked, her voice soft, "What have we stumbled into here?"

"A nightmare," Lott said. "Actually a lot of nightmares for a lot of innocent women and their families."

CALLING DEAD

DEAD

A COLD POKER GANG MYSTERY

DEAN WESLEY SMITH

*wmg*PUBLISHING

Calling Dead

Published 2015 by WMG Publishing
www.wmgpublishing.com
First published in a different form in *Smith's Monthly #18,* March, 2015
Cover and layout copyright © 2015 by WMG Publishing
Cover design by Allyson Longueira/WMG Publishing
Cover art copyright © Andreistancu/Dreamstime
ISBN-13: 978-1-56146-641-2
ISBN-10: 1-56146-641-7

For Kris.
Thanks for all the positive support while I battled this to the end.

CALLING DEAD

A COLD POKER GANG MYSTERY

Calling Dead:
A poker term referring to when a player calls a bet that the player has no chance of winning.

PART ONE

THE DEAL

PROLOGUE

AUGUST 7TH, 2000
9:30 A.M.
IN THE DESERT OUTSIDE OF LAS VEGAS, NEVADA

DETECTIVE BAYARD LOTT stood in the old mine tunnel, staring at the eleven dead women sitting in a neat row on the dirt floor in front of him. Lott had his hands on his hips and was doing his best to keep his breathing level.

And failing.

Not easy. Not easy at all with such a horrific sight.

The tunnel was supported by square and rough wooden pillars about a foot or so apart and not much more than six feet over the hard-dirt floor. The timbers looked old and very dry and some had visible rot on the edges. Dirt and dust filtered down in around the timbers with almost every sound.

It felt to Lott as if the entire thing might come down at any moment. He had always hated enclosed, tight spaces, and this mine was not helping that hatred in any way.

In fact, what he wanted to do was just turn and get out of there, but the bodies in front of him made that impossible.

He was only ten paces inside the boarded-up entrance. The light from the bright day outside helped his flashlight illuminate the scene clearly, while at the same time casting strange and odd-shaped deep black shadows that made the dead women seem even more horrific, if that was possible.

The heat had to be over a hundred inside the tunnel and the air felt used and contaminated with the death he faced. He was sweating, even though the August day outside hadn't gotten that hot yet. It would, later in the afternoon. He couldn't imagine staying in this mine very long now, let alone in the high heat of the desert summer day.

He knew that going deeper underground was cooler, but not this close to the surface in this kind of intense desert heat. This felt more like the interior of a closed-up car.

The smell was like a musty dry cloth that had gone sour. The stench clogged everything in Lott's senses, which was part of why he was breathing through his mouth instead of his nose.

Beside him, his partner, Detective Andor Williams, took slow, loud breaths through his mouth as well.

Andor was shorter than Lott's six feet by five inches, but was a bit wider. Standing side-by-side, they almost touched both sides of the mine walls with their shoulders. Lott's head was only a few inches under the closest timber holding up the dirt above and he had walked bent over to just get this far inside.

Now, seeing what was in here, neither one of them had wanted to take a step farther than what they had already done.

On the dirt floor in front of Lott, sitting with their backs against the left wall of the tunnel, legs stretched out on the dirt, were the eleven dead women. The women were mummified in the heat after clearly being in here for some time, their faces contorted and sunken-in with wrinkles that made them look ancient.

Lott had no doubt that the heat and the tunnel environment was going to make it hell to determine how long these poor women had been in this mine.

It might have been only weeks, but it could have been years. After decades of working as a cop in Las Vegas, Lott had seen heat do some amazing things to a dead human body, so the physical condition of the bodies was no surprise to him.

But what they wore was what surprised him.

Each woman had a black clutch purse on her lap, and her mummified hands covered the purse. Each woman was fully dressed in identical black skirts and white blouses, just sitting with their backs to the wall.

If that wasn't strange enough, they all had long dark hair, trimmed to exactly the same length and in exactly the same style. That, combined with the schoolgirl look of all of them, made the scene look more like a bunch of large wrinkled dolls sitting there instead of women.

Thankfully, all had their eyes closed.

"This is one sick mother who did this," Andor said softly.

Lott could only agree. He had no doubt this sight was going to give him nightmares for a very long time.

"Let's back out of here until forensics can clear the place," Lott said. "If we're lucky, we can just work off the pictures they take."

More than anything, he wanted to be out of that closed-in space and away from the dead women. As a detective, he had seen a lot of death and he had never gotten used to it.

Andor nodded and turned to head back to the mine entrance ten steps away. "Let's just hope the sick bastard who did this left the identifications of those women in those purses."

Lott took one more look back at the eleven dead women, their skin mummified, all dressed like a class of schoolgirls from a very strict school with a uniform dress code.

Horrific didn't begin to describe the scene.

He turned to follow his partner back out into the warm and cleansing desert sunshine. He had a hunch that nothing about this case was going to be easy.

And that hunch proved to be very accurate.

CHAPTER ONE

FIFTEEN YEARS LATER

AUGUST 6TH, 2015
5:30 P.M.
LAS VEGAS

RETIRED DETECTIVE BAYARD LOTT sat at his wooden kitchen table working at a piece of Kentucky Fried Chicken. He loved the legs and always ordered extra legs when he picked up a bucket of KFC for dinner before the weekly poker game he held in his basement poker room. The open bucket now sat in the middle of his table smelling wonderful.

For Lott, there was nothing like fresh KFC.

It made the daily exercise he did to keep his sixty-three-year-old body in shape worthwhile to be able to eat KFC like this regularly.

He would have the chicken for dinner tonight, lunch tomorrow, and maybe a snack or two over the next few days before buying another bucket. His fridge was never without KFC for long.

Across the table from him was his former partner, retired Detective Andor Williams. Beside Andor was retired Reno Detective Julia Rogers. Both Andor and Julia were working at the bucket of chicken as well, making sure Lott didn't have that many days of snacks from this particular bucket.

Tonight, Julia had on a white blouse with a running bra under it and light tan slacks and tennis shoes. Her long brown hair was pulled back and tied off her face and her green eyes seemed to light up with every bite off a chicken wing.

Lott had on a short-sleeved golf shirt and jeans and tennis shoes. Andor wore what he always did, a long-sleeved shirt with the sleeves rolled up and tan slacks and brown dress shoes.

They each had a paper plate, a stack of napkins, and both Andor and Julia had grease on their faces at the moment. Lott had no doubt he did as well.

Julia looked wonderful, even with grease on her face. She exercised as much as he did, if not more, just so she could eat what she wanted as well.

The newly remodeled kitchen echoed the sounds of the three of them working at the dripping, Original-Recipe KFC. The rest of the groceries and snacks for the Cold Poker Gang poker game tonight in the basement were forgotten for the moment on the new granite counter.

Chicken had to come first, especially if it was fresh KFC. That was the rule in his house.

Lott loved the Thursday night games when five or six retired detectives got together to play cards in his downstairs poker room.

While playing, they also worked on and talked about cold cases for the Las Vegas police department.

Even though they were all retired, a few years back the chief of police had given the Cold Poker Gang special unit status. That was because the Cold Poker Gang had solved some of the city's most puzzling cold cases.

All of the gang could still carry their guns and badges, but they didn't get paid and weren't officially on the force.

But that was enough for all of them to feel valued. And after closing so many major cold cases, everyone on the force, including the chief of police, gave them all a lot of respect, which Lott liked more than he wanted to admit.

Sometimes in retirement, all you had to live on was respect. Past or present.

He would take either.

And they all knew they were lucky. Even after retirement, they got to continue a job they all loved and had lived their lives to do. But they didn't have to do all the paperwork or report at certain hours. They worked at their own pace and on their own time and money.

Julia called it "Retirement with benefits."

Lott's daughter Annie, also a former Las Vegas Detective, had found that extremely funny, but the humor had just gone right past Lott. Julia had promised she would explain at some point, which made Annie laugh all the harder.

As far as Lott was concerned, this was a perfect job, even though he didn't get paid for it. The job had value, made him feel valued, something that didn't come easy in retirement.

He had been forced to retire early, at fifty-nine, before he had wanted. He had decided to be with Carol, his wife, during her last year of sickness. She had now been gone for four years, and Lott was finally moving on with his life, thanks to the Cold Poker Gang, his daughter, Annie, and Julia beside him.

Julia had been forced to retire from the Reno police department at the age of fifty-five when a bullet shattered her leg. She barely had a limp, but the injury had been too much to allow her to continue working, so she had moved to Las Vegas to be close to her daughter, Jane, and play some poker.

It was during a poker tournament out on the Strip that Julia had met Annie and learned about the Cold Poker Gang. Julia was the only woman in the gang at the moment.

But Lott knew that two of the best women detectives still active on the force were thinking of retiring soon, and both wanted to join the gang. It would be great to have them in the game.

And to help with the cases.

Julia and Lott had hit it off almost at once after she joined the game just over a year ago. They were slowly building a solid relationship. He now often spent the night at her condo and loved waking up beside her in the mornings.

She and Andor made it a habit to come over early on game nights and help him eat KFC and set up the downstairs poker room.

It was during the game that Andor presented cold cases he had gotten from the chief of police for the gang to work on. They only got a new case when they had solved an earlier one, or had given up on one.

Actually, they never gave up on a case, they just put the file "on the bar" near the poker table downstairs to be reviewed every week. They were all very proud of the fact that in over two years of doing this, only five files were "on the bar."

They had closed a lot of very cold cases.

"So what's the new case tonight?" Julia asked Andor, giving him a smile that could melt most anyone. She blinked her large green eyes at Andor who just shook his head.

"Nice try, Rogers," Andor said, then took a bite on another piece of chicken.

Lott laughed. Andor always kept the cases secret until after an hour into the game. Then he would present them like presenting a gift to a royal court. She asked him ahead every time there was a new case, and he never told her. It was a little dance they both seemed to enjoy.

Andor was a bulldog of a human being. He never walked anywhere. He stormed. He had a heart of gold, but a bull exterior. Julia was thin and not much taller than Andor. She moved around him like a butterfly around a stump. Sometimes that drove Andor crazy, but Lott knew Andor really liked and admired Julia.

Andor had also had been forced to retire early to take care of his wife, who had died just six months after Carol had died. Lott and Andor had spent a lot of those months after Andor's wife died sitting in bars drinking.

It did neither of them any good, but it was the only thing they could think to do at the time.

The Cold Poker Gang had gotten both of them back to work, and they loved it.

"All I will tell you about the new case," Andor said, licking off his fingers and dropping the bones of the chicken on his plate, "is that today is the fifteenth anniversary of the day Lott and I originally caught the case."

Andor glanced at Lott and shrugged, almost an apology before going back to work on yet another piece of chicken.

Lott stared at his former partner.

Fifteen years would make the year of the case 2000. Early August. What cases had they done at that time that went cold? They hadn't had that many cases go cold over the years. Maybe ten major ones was all and they have already solved a couple of those with the gang.

Then Lott suddenly realized which case Andor was talking about. And why he had given him that apologetic look.

"You are kidding, right?" Lott asked.

Andor shook his head. "About damn time we give those eleven women some justice, don't you think?"

Lott dropped the drumstick on his plate, wiped off his hands and sat back. He hated this idea.

He hated it more than he wanted to think about.

He had hated that case more than any other case they had caught over the years. It had given him nightmares for years, and there hadn't been a clue that seemed to lead them anywhere to who had killed the women.

He had woken up Carol on more than one night by screaming in a nightmare when that case was active.

It was the coldest of the cold cases they had.

Julia glanced at him, clearly seeing he was upset.

"That bad?" she asked.

Both Andor and Lott nodded.

"A case of nightmares," Lott said.

"In more ways than one," Andor said.

"Damn, I hate this idea," Lott said.

"Yeah, me too," Andor said. "But we need to do it."

CHAPTER TWO

———

THE TWENTY-FOUR HOUR café at the Bellagio was busy, but not so crowded at almost midnight that they couldn't get one of their favorite booths tucked back in a corner and surrounded by tall green plants. The sounds of the slots in the casino was nothing more than a background noise. The low murmur of people talking and laughing filled the air.

Julia loved casinos, loved the energy, loved the feel. And she flat adored the food in this café. Anything she wanted to eat at any hour of the day or night, and top quality at a decent price. Didn't get better.

Especially after a long night of poker.

She enjoyed coming here after the Cold Poker Gang games with Lott. And tonight she had asked Andor to join them. She had really, really wanted to get more information on the cold case he had brought to the table tonight. And since Lott and Andor had been the two lead detectives on the cold case fifteen years before, they knew more than anyone.

The case had been called "The School Girl Murders" because of the way the woman were dressed and placed in the cave. To Julia, the entire thing sounded grisly and yet fascinating. She could not have imagined walking into that mine with those bodies like Lott and Andor had done.

But the entire case had the feeling of something far, far larger. And she didn't know why.

Lott had come into the casino near the poker room to tell his daughter, Annie, and her boyfriend, Doc Hill, that he and Julia would be in the café.

So she had managed to beat Lott to the booth by only a minute and Andor was yet to be seen.

"They still in the tournament?" Julia asked as Lott slid into the large booth beside her and took his cloth napkin and put it on his lap. She knew that Annie and Doc played in a major tournament here every week. Annie was also a retired Las Vegas detective, but she had retired to play poker full time and was now considered one of the best female poker players in the country.

Doc was considered the best no-limit hold'em tournament poker player there was. Period. Julia considered herself a good player and had won her share of small tournaments, but compared to Annie and Doc, she was still a beginner.

"Both still in the tournament," Lott said, taking a sip of the glass of water the waitress had brought. "Annie has a stack and Doc is short-chipped, but I have a hunch that won't last long. Three tables left, so they have a ways to go yet."

Julia nodded.

At that point, Andor joined them, sliding into the booth across the dark-colored table to face them.

"Hungry," he said, grabbing a menu from where the hostess had left them on the front edge. Not hi, nothing.

After they finished deciding what to order and gave the smiling waitress with blonde hair tucked up on her head their order, Julia looked first at Lott, then at Andor.

"All right," she said. "What's not in that file you two aren't talking about?"

Andor just shook his head and beside her Lott sighed.

Then Lott said, "We had eleven women, all in their mid-thirties, all with long black hair cut to the same length."

"And all dressed the same," Julia said, shuddering a little and glad they were in the bright, alive casino. Those pictures Andor had brought with him had been just like a bad horror movie.

Andor nodded, so Lott went on.

"We found the identities of nine of the eleven women," Lott said, "as was in the file. They were abducted about one per month for almost a year. The best anyone could figure, they had been in the cave for two years. We never did find information about the other two I'm afraid."

"And no connection at all between the women?" Julia asked.

"None that we could find," Andor said. "Except that they all had natural black hair. And the school uniforms they were dressed in were standard and could be bought anywhere in the country at the time."

"File says no DNA," Julia said. "Any chance fifteen years and better technology would make a difference on that?"

Andor shook his head.

"All the women were cleaned perfectly," Lott said.

"How did they die?" Julia said. "I didn't see that in the file."

Andor glanced at Lott, then looked at Julia. "We kept it out of the file to use if we needed it."

Julia knew that was standard. Every department did that.

"They basically died of dehydration and heat," Lott said.

"Slowly," Andor said. "There was no indication that any of the women struggled at all, so more than likely they were drugged and then died from the heat."

"In the cave?" Julia asked, shocked.

Lott shook his head.

Andor stared at the table.

"They were left to die somewhere in the heat?" Julia asked. She didn't know what she felt about that. Only a true monster would do that.

"Not really, no," Andor said. "They weren't just left in the heat."

"They were baked," Lott said

"Baked?" Julia asked, turning to stare at the very troubled face of the man she had come to love over the last year. Baked made no sense at all. How could you bake a human being?

Lott nodded.

"Best we can figure," Andor said. "They were slipped into a huge oven on some sort of surface that would not conduct heat. Then they were baked, first on one side, then on the other. Slowly."

"Very slowly," Lott said, clearly disgusted. "Not hot enough to blister the skin, but hot enough to dry them out like a raisin over time."

"Oh, my god," Julia said. She was having trouble even trying to imagine such a thing, or one human doing that to another.

"Then the sick bastard dressed them, trimmed their hair, and staged them in the cave," Lott said.

Julia shook her head, trying to push the image of a naked woman baking in an oven out of her mind. "That's going to give me nightmares."

"Welcome to the club," Andor said.

"And that's not the worst part," Lott said.

"There's something worse than baking a woman alive?" Julia asked, now really, really sorry that she had been interested beyond the game earlier.

Andor stared at the table in front of him, then he said simply, "The guy liked flank steak."

"Rump roast as well," Lott said.

"Yeah," Andor said. "All the good parts."

CHAPTER THREE

THE FOOD CAME at that moment, the waitress carrying a large round tray on her shoulder and putting it down on a stand beside the table. Lott was glad that they had all decided to not talk about the cold case while eating. That case was just not good dinner conversation.

The possibility of cannibalism just put most sane people right off their food.

By the time they mostly finished eating, Annie walked up. She was frowning and had what Lott recognized as a "bad beat" cloud over her head.

She had on a dark blue blouse and jeans and had her brown hair pulled back off her face. Like her mother, Carol, Annie was tall and thin and always walked with a purpose.

She slid in beside Andor, shaking her head.

"Thought you had a large stack," Lott said. "What happened?"

"Pair of nines cracked my aces," Annie said, "and then I couldn't get ace-king to hold up."

"Ouch," Lott said.

"Yeah, double ouch," Julia said. "Doc still in?"

"He is and it's a thing of beauty to watch at times," Annie said, shaking her head. "But after those two beats, I needed to get something to eat."

"Well," Lott said, smiling at his beautiful daughter, "we're happy to have you."

A moment later the waitress came to take some of their dirty dishes and Annie's order.

"So what's the new case tonight?" Annie asked. "A fun one?"

"Not so fun tonight," Andor said.

"Gross, actually," Julia said.

"The School Girl Murders," Lott said. "We're giving that case another run."

Annie looked at him surprised. "The cannibal case? Really?"

"We don't know the guy was a cannibal," Lott said.

"We don't even know it was a guy for sure," Andor said. "In fact, we flat know nothing."

"Fifteen years and not a clue has surfaced," Lott said. "Cold as a dark day in the winter in Antarctica."

"Wow," Annie said. "So refresh me on the case and let's set a plan of attack."

Lott laughed. "You want to help on this one?"

"I was still a patrol officer when this one came in," Annie said. "Always sort of held a fascination for me."

"Gave me nightmares," Andor said. "But glad to have any help on this monster."

So for the next few minutes they went over again what was in the file and the knowledge that wasn't common, such as the slow baking of the bodies to kill the women, and then the removal of some of the body's meat.

Lott was feeling a little more settled about taking on the case again. He was putting it back into perspective. This all was done by a sick serial killer who needed to be caught and punished if he was still alive after all this time.

"So let's list the clear points we have to go on," Julia said, pulling out a notebook from her purse and opening it to a blank page.

"School girl obsession," Andor said. "Those uniforms were mostly used for grades seven through twelve. Usually in Catholic and some private schools."

Julia nodded and wrote that down. Then she looked at Lott. "You said the women were abducted at a pace of about one per month?"

"They were," Lott said. "Two years before we found the bodies."

"Nothing at all similar with the women. Some were rich, some single, some married. All had black hair."

"So black hair a certain length is an obsession as well," Julia said, writing that down.

"I wonder why the killer stopped at eleven," Annie said. "Is there something about the number eleven that might be a lead?"

Lott nodded as Julia wrote that down as well. He remembered that he and Andor had thought of that, but could find no connection at all. But never hurt to look again.

"So how could a human body be baked?" Julia asked. "Was one side or the other burned?"

"No burns," Lott said. "Just really slow baked and the fluids drained off.

"We tried to figure that out as well," Andor said. "The bodies must have been put on something that wouldn't transmit heat, some sort of pad or something, then put in a very large oven."

"Actually they were still alive when put in the oven," Lott said. "But drugged. Since all the blood was gone when we found them, basically either drained out or evaporated from the heat. Add onto that the two years that had passed in the cave and we never did determine what that drug might have been."

That stopped the four retired detectives cold. Standard for this case. No real leads at all.

Julia wrote in her notebook, but Lott didn't try to follow what she was writing. She was good at sometimes putting pieces together that others didn't see. This case was going to take a miracle of pieces and some real luck to solve.

After a few moments, the waitress brought Annie her Denver omelet with white toast and coffee. Even though Lott had just eaten a Chef's Salad, the omelet smelled good.

Lott wasn't convinced he could eat and talk about this topic, even though it had been years and he was working to get some distance on the topic.

"So after they were baked," Julia said, looking at the paper in front of her, "the killer cut off slices of meat from each woman?"

Lott nodded.

"So the assumption was that the killer was a cannibal," Julia said.

"That's where all the jokes around the force went," Andor said. "But we have no evidence of what the killer did with the cuts of meat from the bodies. He could have fed them to zoo animals for all we know."

"I can't remember," Annie said, working at the omelet. "How did you find the bodies in that old mine? Wasn't it boarded up?"

Lott laughed. "A psychic called it in, saying she was having night-mares, seeing a class of girls sitting in the heat in an old mine."

Julia looked at him. "You're serious?"

"Betty?" Annie asked.

"Betty," Lott said, smiling at Julia. "We used her all the time, off the books, of course."

"She was damned good," Andor said. "But never quote me on that."

Julia just shook her head. "Can this case get any stranger?"

"We just started investigating it again," Lott said. "So who knows?"

"Oh, great, just great," Andor said. "I may never sleep again."

CHAPTER FOUR

"SO WHAT KIND of oven would be large enough to bake a human body without burning it?" Annie asked between bites of her omelet.

Julia nodded and quickly wrote that question down as well. She liked how Annie thought. Actually, she liked Annie period. She was an amazing woman, and very accepting of Julia being with her father. She seemed to know that Julia would never try to replace Annie's mother.

"We figured it was a commercial bread oven," Andor said.

"Or a pizza oven," Lott said. "We checked the bread ovens and they pretty much have a crew on them twenty-four-seven. Pizza ovens were another matter."

"I think we found something like sixty-five pizza ovens in the Las Vegas area," Andor said, "all large enough to hold a human body full inside while on some sort of protective padding."

"Nothing came of that, I assume," Annie said.

"Nothing," Lott said.

Julia wrote that down as well. Something was bothering her and that bit of information finally brought it out. "So why go to the bother of baking the women before taking the meat? Wouldn't that just dry the desired meat out?"

Lott shrugged. "We asked ourselves that same question."

Andor laughed. "Lott even had Carol put in a roast and bake it at a slow temperature without water like a pizza oven would bake it."

"Dried up so bad," Lott said, "that when I cut it, it was so dry, I just marinated the strips I cut and put it into the food dehydrator to make jerky."

"You never told Mom the reason you were doing that, did you?" Annie asked, looking shocked.

Julia and Andor laughed.

"I never said a word as to why," Lott said. "I promise. But she thought I had lost a marble or two for wasting a perfectly good roast like that."

"So back to my question," Julia said. "Clearly baking the women has some meaning to our killer, just as the clothing and the number of victims does. He decided to actually kill them by baking them. That has to mean something."

"I'm betting it does," Annie said.

"And maybe the mine shaft as well," Lott said.

"We didn't even look much at that angle," Andor said. "The mine was owned by a mining corporation that was as surprised as anyone to discover what their closed mine had been used for."

Julia nodded and wrote that all down. Lots of pieces, no idea what the puzzle even looked like. But there was something else really bothering her, so she just blurted it out.

"Why did this killer stop?"

Beside her Lott shrugged and Andor shook his head.

"We're not sure the killer did stop," Lott said. "For years after finding the bodies, which was two years after they were put into the mine, we searched for any references to anything similar anywhere. Nothing came up."

"So we need to do that search again," Annie said. "I'll get Fleet and his team of computer experts on that. They should be able to easily find any sort of reference to this kind of thing if it came up anywhere in the world."

"Thanks," Lott said. "That will help."

Fleet was Annie's boyfriend's best friend. Doc and Fleet had been partners since they had both been in college, with Doc earning massive amounts of money from poker, and Fleet making very wise investments and building a vast corporation of holdings. Right now they were both so rich, they almost felt embarrassed to talk about it.

But Fleet had a computer crew that could get any information without being caught or seen. Annie had met Doc when Doc and Fleet were after the man who had killed Doc's father, and eventually would kill the White House Chief of Staff. That case had forced them to set up a very deep network of computer experts, and they had kept the team together.

Doc and Annie and their team now helped the FBI a great deal on different cases, including one that Lott and Julia had been involved in just lately, stopping one of the worst serial killers of all time.

"My nightmare," Andor said, "is for the last fifteen years, this killer has just continued in this area unchecked."

"That many women haven't gone missing in Las Vegas, have they?" Annie asked.

"Not in Las Vegas," Andor said. "But the women we identified in that cave were from five different states."

That made Julia's stomach twist hard. A killer who went out to get his victims was even harder to trace.

Julia hoped the killer was long gone. Because if not, a lot of woman had died an ugly death over the last fifteen years.

She looked over at Annie. "Can you have Fleet and his computer friends do one other search?"

Annie nodded, her eyes dark and very serious. "You thinking he should look for more black-haired women who have gone missing around Nevada and in all the neighboring states?"

"Exactly," Julia said. "Make the search pattern the entire western half of the country."

"Damn I hope you are wrong about that being possible," Lott said.

"So do I," Julia said. "And I'm sure I am. But we got to check."

CHAPTER FIVE

AUGUST 7TH, 2015
10:45 A.M.
LAS VEGAS

LOTT SAT AT Julia's small wooden kitchen table, sipping coffee and trying to wake up after a restless night. The kitchen window beside the table looked out over the condo complex's lawn and pool and was very calming. There was no one in the dozen lounge chairs around the pool at the moment.

Bringing back the case had certainly made sleeping difficult, even with Julia beside him. But the sun of mid-morning streaming in the window was helping some, along with the coffee.

Julia's condo's kitchen was small, but functional and comfortable. It was partially open to a larger dining room over a granite counter, but he and Julia liked the small wooden table tucked off to one side of the kitchen in front of the window.

The view out the small kitchen window was calming, if calming was possible when dealing with this case. Lott figured he would take anything he could get when it came to calm at the moment.

The coffee he had made was a French roast and tasted rich. It was Julia's favorite kind, and he had a hunch she was going to need it. She had tossed and turned more than normal during the night, and looked tired when she kissed him good morning and headed for the shower.

He had already showered ahead of her and made coffee and now worked at a bowl of Raisin Bran. But he couldn't finish it all. The dried raisins just kept bringing him back to how those poor women's skin looked while sitting in that mine.

He had hated this case when they had caught it the first time. He was starting to hate it just as much with this second look. And they hadn't even been at it for a full day yet.

Just as he pushed the half-finished bowl of cereal aside, Julia came in looking refreshed, her skin glowing from the shower, a faint smell of lotion around her. She had on a thin white blouse with a sports bra under it and jeans.

He watched her, marveling at how lucky he was to have met her as she poured herself a cup of coffee and put in some toast before kissing him good morning and sitting down beside him. She was the most beautiful woman he had ever met, of that he had no doubt.

After Carol died, he had never figured he would ever move on. Carol had been the love of his life and his partner in life for decades. But now, four years later, he wasn't replacing Carol. He was just starting something new with Julia.

"Long night?" he asked.

"Up twice to make some notes," Julia said. "If that pervert is still out there, we have to stop him."

"I agree," he said, smiling. Detectives just never let a case go. Carol used to complain that he couldn't stop working on a case even at breakfast. Now clearly, Julia was the same way he was.

"So what did you think of that got you out of bed?" Lott asked.

"The mine," she said, turning around and grabbing a small notebook from the white counter top that separated the small kitchen from the dining area. "That mine bothered me last night and it is bothering me still."

Lott leaned forward watching as she took a sip of coffee and then sighed at the wonderful taste. If it was possible, she became more beautiful when focused.

"You think the mine company has something to do with this?" he asked. "Andor and I just didn't spend that much time on it, to be honest."

At that moment, the toast popped up and she stood to get it and put some butter and strawberry jam on the two pieces.

"The stuff with my ex-husband made me realize that often mining companies can hide some pretty amazing things."

"Very true," he said. "And Nevada sure has no shortages of old mines to hide things in."

She brought her toast over and sat down, taking a bite before looking at her notebook. Then she said, "My second idea was that maybe there was a mine tragedy at some point where eleven girls in a class were killed. Did you try to research that?"

Lott sat back, surprised. "No, we didn't, but I'll call Annie and have her get Fleet and his wizards on it."

At that moment Lott's cell phone buzzed in his shirt pocket. He had turned off the ringer for the night. He pulled the phone out.

"Speaking of Annie," Lott said, holding the phone up to the smiling Julia.

He clicked on the phone, glad that Annie had called. "Up early this morning, daughter."

"Got some bad news," Annie said, her voice sounding about as serious as it could be. "It didn't take Fleet and his crew more than a few hours to track over three hundred missing women who matched the profile of the women in the mine. He ran the search from two years before you found the women to now."

Lott felt his stomach twist into a tight knot. "Three hundred?"

Julia's eyes across the table grew wide in a look of horror.

"Afraid so," Annie said. "Fleet has his people running advanced programs on all of them to see if there are similar details among them besides the initial look. Or if there was a more likely reason they went missing. He's also looking for any similarities, such as a make of a car seen close by or things like that. But that's going to take some time."

"How wide an area did he search?" Lott asked.

"All of Montana, Colorado, New Mexico and every state west," Annie said.

"All basically a two day drive from the Las Vegas area," Lott said.

"Pretty much," Annie said. "Not all of these women who are missing will be involved, of course. But if our killer did eleven women a year for the last fifteen years, that's over a hundred and fifty women."

Lott had no idea what to say to that.

Nothing at all.

"We've got to find this sicko," Annie said.

"We will," Lott said. "We're not letting this one go. Two more things that Julia came up with to have Fleet research."

"Fire away," Annie said. "After finding that number this morning, Doc and Fleet are all in with this investigation. Whatever we need, they are willing to throw time, money, and resources at this."

"Good to hear," Lott said. "First off, have Fleet and his people do deep background on the mining company that owned that first mine. Find out how many other mines they own that are closed up around the Las Vegas area and where they are and so on."

"Got it," Annie said.

"And see if Fleet can go back in time and find an incident when a group of school kids died in a mine, or some sort of heat accident. Basically eleven of them, all girls. Something triggered this behavior."

"Tell Julia those are great ideas," Annie said. "Talk with you soon."

She hung up and Lott sort of stared at his phone before turning the ringer back on and putting it in his shirt pocket again.

"Over three hundred?" Julia asked.

Lott nodded. "Fleet searched the years since we found the first mine from Montana south to the Mexican border and everything west of that. And with very strict parameters."

Julia just sat there in the warm sun basking the kitchen table, shaking her head, the last of her toast forgotten.

Lott had no idea what to say. There was nothing he could say.

Finally Julia asked, her voice soft, "What have we stumbled into here?"

"A nightmare," Lott said. "Actually a lot of nightmares for a lot of innocent women and their families."

CHAPTER SIX

AUGUST 7TH, 2015
1:45 P.M.
LAS VEGAS

JULIA AND LOTT had talked with Andor and decided to meet for lunch back at the Bellagio Café. Annie said she would meet them.

That way they could all get something decent to eat and plan the next steps in the case. Julia figured they were all going to need to have some good meals while this was going on.

Even with stopping past Lott's place for a change of clothes, Julia and Lott got to the restaurant first, with Lott driving his Cadillac SUV and the air conditioning working at full. The day's temperature had already climbed past 105 and Lott gave the car to the valet so they were only in the heat for less than thirty seconds.

Lott had on jeans, tennis shoes, and a light short-sleeved golf shirt. Julia had pulled her hair back and tied it away from her face. On summer days like this in Vegas, anything extra around her face just made her feel even hotter.

Lott had admitted to her last night that both he and Andor had had nightmares for years about the fact that they had not stopped the killer. And that the killings had been going on.

Now it seemed that nightmare might have been the truth.

They managed, with only a short wait for the table to be cleaned, to get their favorite booth tucked back among the plants along the back wall of the cafe.

Andor joined them five minutes later after they both had iced tea in front of them.

"Do we have a permanent reserved sign on this booth?" Andor asked as he slid in across from them. He had a gleam of sweat on his face and took a napkin and wiped it off. Julia knew that even though he had more than enough money, Andor would never pay for valet service, even on the hottest days.

Both Andor and Lott had lived their entire lives here in Vegas, so they understood the heat. But as Lott had told her a month ago on a really hot day, understanding the heat and liking it were two different things.

Annie joined them a couple minutes later, sliding in beside Andor and putting a gray folder on the table in front of her.

"Where's Doc?" Lott asked.

"He flew up to Boise this morning," Annie said, "after we got the first count on the missing women. He wants to help Fleet and the rest at their corporate office headquarters in the research. Plus, knowing him, he's going to be pulling in favors from law enforcement agencies everywhere if needed."

Julia was very glad to hear that Annie and Doc and Fleet were working on this so hard. They had basically unlimited resources, knew every cop and FBI agent in Idaho and Nevada, and weren't afraid to skirt the law when it came to computer discovery methods.

Annie pushed the folder toward her father. "Fleet and Doc just sent me this. They just found it."

To Julia, Lott looked like he was almost afraid to open it, but he did.

From what Julia could see as she scooted over slightly closer to look at the same time, it was a newspaper article with a picture of a bus stuck on a dirt road among some desert rocks.

"Nineteen eighty-eight," Annie said. "A bus taking a small class of sophomore girls from Saint Mary's, a local Catholic High School, on a desert field trip had engine troubles about thirty miles out in the desert north of here. They were in a small canyon, hidden from view for the most part."

Julia stared at the newspaper article as Annie went on giving a summary of what had happened.

"The missing bus and students became a firestorm over the two days it took to find them, since they were not where they were supposed to be going for the day."

Julia glanced at the article, then decided to wait to read it. She wanted to hear what Annie had found.

"The reporter made some assumptions," Annie said. "The teacher, an older woman, was notoriously deathly afraid of snakes, and more than likely wouldn't allow the girls to leave the bus."

"Oh, shit," Andor said. "On a hot day in the sun, that bus would quickly become an oven."

Annie nodded. "The bus driver and his fourteen-year-old son went for help, but they were turned back by the heat and lack of water.

The reporter and police reports believe that by the time the father and son made it back to the bus, the eleven girls were all passed out. The older-aged teacher was dead."

Julia could feel her stomach twisting just listening to this horror story.

"Somehow," Annie said, "the report believes that the father and the son managed to carry the girls out of the bus and up a small hill to an old mine. The mine was a little cooler and they put the girls in there, sitting up against the wall of the tunnel."

"Eleven school girls all dressed the same in a mine," Andor said, shaking his head. "Now we know where all this started."

"There's more," Annie said, looking grim. "The father left the boy and went for help. The father didn't make it, passed out near a high-way and died. It was a full day before anyone found his body, and then found the girls. They were all dead. Only the boy survived. He was on the verge of death."

"I'll bet," Andor said.

Annie took a deep breath and then said, "He had removed all the girl's panties and had them in his pocket."

The silence at the table was so intense, Julia wondered if the casino had shut down around them.

Finally Andor said, "So we're looking for the kid. If he was four-teen in 1988, he would have been twenty-six when we found the bodies."

"And over forty now," Lott said.

Julia forced herself to take a deep breath and then sip her iced tea. At that moment, the waitress came by, a woman with a high voice, a big smile, and artificially built-up breasts under her white uniform blouse. She took Annie's and Andor's drink orders, then all of their food orders.

That time allowed Julia to get back centered after listening to that horrid story. Sometimes, even as a detective, stories got to her, and the image of eleven school girls baking to death in a school bus was going to be hard to clear from her mind.

"So what's the kid's name?"

"It used to be Kirk Wampler," Annie said. "But it seems his father was his only relative and when the father died, Kirk was put into the system and just vanished."

"Vanished?" Andor asked before Julia could. "It was damn hard, if not impossible for a kid to vanish into the Child Protective Services in this state. Run away, yes, but not just vanish."

"That's what Fleet and his people call it," Annie said, "but they are looking and we have a few family names to go visit here in this area that he was put with right after his father's death. They might be able to give us some hints as to what happened to Kirk."

"So we're looking at Kirk to be the one for this?" Lott asked.

He glanced at Andor, who nodded.

Then Lott looked at Julia.

"I think he's our best lead at the moment," Julia said.

Lott smiled. "I could hear a 'but' there."

Julia was impressed. Lott was already getting to know her more than anyone before had ever done. And she was letting him and liking it, honestly.

Julia tapped the folder with the story in it that Annie had relayed. "I believe this incident, if it happened as reported here, started all this. We have to make sure this actually happened as reported. Seems to me there is a lot of guessing in this report."

"A hell of a lot," Andor said.

"Fleet and his people are working on that," Annie said, nodding in agreement.

"I'll get in touch with the chief and pull the official reports on the case and on the search," Andor said. "See if anything was left out of the official story that we would need to know."

Julia nodded. "What bothers me is that this just seems a little too pat for my tastes, all aiming directly at Kirk. There are a lot of others who were hurt by this incident. For example, all the parents, all the brothers and sisters who lost a family member. And so on. Something like this could knock anyone over an edge."

Lott nodded and smiled. "Looks like we have a ton of work ahead of us on this."

"But at least we have some leads now," Andor said. "Damn that feels good after all these years."

And with that, Julia could only agree.

CHAPTER SEVEN

AUGUST 7TH, 2015
3:45 P.M.
LAS VEGAS

LOTT PARKED HIS Cadillac SUV just down the block from the home that had taken Kirk Wampler after the accident and his father dying. Lott left the car running for a moment to keep the air conditioning pouring cool air over them. Outside the official temperature had climbed to over a hundred and seven. No telling what it was on this street.

Beside him Julia sighed, but said nothing. She clearly wasn't looking forward to this any more than he was.

It seemed Kirk had gone into some treatment after the accident at a hospital for a few months before being released to this family. It was amazing any family would take him after his history and at fourteen.

The house was a sprawling, single-story brown stucco that needed some tender-loving care and a new coat of paint. The lawn was not only completely brown, but looked like it had gone to dirt years before. Two large green garbage cans sat near the closed garage door, both overflowing.

It didn't look much different, actually, than the other houses along this street off the old Boulder Highway. This neighborhood had seen much better days, of that there was no doubt.

No trees or even small shrubs were around the house or any of the closest homes. The drapes in every home were pulled tight. One barren and lifeless place, that's for sure.

Lott knew the look of this home. More than likely this family took the kids in the system just for the money. And they did just a good enough job with the kids to keep getting more. Any kid tossed into the foster care system never really got much of a break.

Kirk had vanished from all records after being with this family for just under a year. Lott hoped he and Julia might find some sort of trace of where he had gone.

"Ready?" Lott asked Julia glancing at her. The air conditioning was blowing slight wisps of hair back from her face and she had a very worried look.

"Is anyone ever ready for this kind of thing?" Julia asked, staring at the home they were going to visit.

"Never," Lott said, smiling.

"Then let's go," she said, opening her door and climbing out.

He laughed and shut off the car and climbed out into the blast-furnace heat, moving to the front of the car to stand beside her. On the pavement like this, the temperature had to be well past one hundred and ten and climbing.

At a decent speed, they headed for the home's front door. Both of them were armed and Lott had his badge ready as well to flash.

They banged on the front door since it was clear the remains of an old doorbell were long past working.

After fifteen extremely hot seconds waiting as the heat not only radiated from the porch, but off the side of the building, someone pulled the door open.

"Yeah," the woman who answered said from the shadows. The smell of bacon hit them through a rough screen door as well as some hints of cooler air.

Lott flashed his badge, holding it up for the woman to see. "Detectives Lott and Rogers. Mrs. Mitchell, we would like to talk with you for a moment about a boy you once fostered by the name of Kirk Wampler."

"You're kidding, right?" the woman asked. Then she pushed the door open and indicated they should come in.

Inside the door was an entry area with empty hooks on the wall. Just beyond the entry was a big living room that looked to be an organized zone of clutter. Toys for small kids were scattered near a large wooden toy box, but not much distance from the box. A card table with a puzzle half put together was in front of a couch facing a large-screen television. And the entire place was dark and cool, something Lott very much appreciated at that moment.

Mitchell was a thin woman, not much taller than five feet, with gray hair pulled back into a bun of sorts, and an apron covering jeans and a dark blouse. From what Lott could find out from a quick call, she and her husband, a dentist, had been fostering kids for over twenty years and seemed to be good at what they did and clearly didn't need the money from doing foster care even though their home looked like they did.

She had on flip-flops and far too much makeup. She didn't indicate that they should sit down, so the three of them stood there on the scarred wooden entrance floor.

"Why you interested in Kirk after all this time?"

"His name came up in a cold case we were working on," Julia said, giving the woman a smile. "Just trying to figure out what happened to Kirk after he left here. He seemed to have vanished from the system."

Mitchell laughed, a sort of rough laugh that had no warmth at all to it.

"I suppose that case is about what happened to his dad and those poor girls in that mine, right?"

Lott nodded.

"It is," Julia said.

"Poor kid never really got over that, even after a couple months with professional help," Mitchell said.

Lott was surprised. Mitchell actually sounded sad.

"So what was he like?" Julia asked.

Mitchell shrugged. "Kept to himself, quiet, didn't much like school. Real depressed. Not a damn thing my husband or I could do to change that and let me tell you, we tried. Near the end here the doctors from the hospital had him on some anti-depressants of some sort, but it did no good."

"See any signs of other problems with him?" Lott asked.

Mitchell shook her head. "Stayed in his room all the time when not forced to come out and eat or go to school."

"So you have any idea where he went after here?" Julia asked.

Mitchell kind of jerked back, then shook her head. "The doctors said they were going to keep it quiet, guess they did."

Lott wasn't liking the sound of this at all. "Keep what quiet?"

"Kirk killed himself," Mitchell said.

Lott could see the hurt in her eyes. This woman actually did care for the kids she was trying to help.

"How did he do that?" Julia asked, her voice soft.

"He stepped out in front of an empty school bus. He's buried beside his mom and dad up in the Palm Cemetery off the beltway."

Lott felt like he was going to be sick. It was a school bus trip that had gone horribly wrong and killed his dad and those girls. And it had ended up killing Kirk as well.

They thanked Mitchell and apologized for bothering her and headed back out into the heat.

Their best lead was dead.

And now all Lott could ask himself was what next?

Chapter Eight

August 7th, 2015
4:45 p.m.
Las Vegas

LOTT HAD DECIDED that the news about Kirk required a fresh bucket of KFC for dinner, even though there was some cold KFC still in the fridge from last night.

Julia liked that idea. She wasn't sure why the news that Kirk was dead had rocked her so much. With so many women missing, she had just hoped that the answer to this craziness would be simple.

But it now looked like it was going to be far, far from simple. They had no leads at all. None. Maybe a hundred possible suspects, but no leads.

While Lott headed them back toward his place through downtown traffic, Julia called first Andor and then Lott's daughter, Annie, and told them of the KFC plans at Lott's house.

"Perfect," Andor had said. "I was starting to grow roots in that booth at the Bellagio."

Annie said she would be there, but she didn't sound upbeat in the slightest. And Julia did not tell her or Andor about Kirk being dead.

They desperately needed some sort of break in this case.

Lott headed into the drive-through at the nearest KFC to his home. They hadn't talked much during the twenty minutes it had taken them to get across town. Not much to talk about, since they were both focused on the case.

But as they waited, Lott turned to her. "From what Mrs. Mitchell said, Kirk had a lot of doctors. I think we need to see if we can get his medical records."

Julia nodded. "I agree. But at this point I'm not sure what good it will do."

She was convinced that the records would show that Kirk was destroyed by survivor guilt and depression from what had happened to his father and those girls. She had seen survivors of some major tragedy or another kill themselves more times than she wanted to admit.

"Those girl's underwear being found in Kirk's pocket bothers me," Lott said, rolling up the window after the woman gave him his change and said it would be a minute.

"Maybe part of the survivor guilt that killed him," Julia said.

"Might be," Lott said, nodding. "Or they were planted there."

Julia was surprised at that statement. "Why would you say that?"

Lott looked at her, his dark eyes clear and intense. "The eleven women we found in the cave also didn't have underwear on. We paid little attention to that fact because of the hunks of flesh gone from the legs and butts of the women. We figured it was just part of the killer cutting them up. But maybe we should have paid attention to the missing underwear."

"Signs of sexual assault at all?" Julia asked, shocked.

Lott only shrugged. "None after the woman were baked. But I was told that kind of baking and mummifying process would pretty much clean out any sign of sexual activity unless the sex was rough and caused damage."

Julia turned and sat back, thinking. "I wonder if the girls in that mine with Kirk were sexually assaulted before or after they died?"

Lott shook his head. "I honestly don't know. Annie didn't say anything about that, but that kind of information would have been withheld."

"I'll call Andor and see if he has managed to dig up the entire file on that case." Julia said. "Every damn hidden detail of it."

Lott nodded and she was on the phone when Lott took the bucket from the woman in the take-out window and the wonderful smell of fresh KFC filled the car.

Andor said he got it all, including all the autopsies of all the girls and the father. Then he asked, "Got the bucket of chicken yet?"

"Sitting between us as I speak," Julia said.

"I knew I could smell something," Andor said and hung up.

She laughed, then glanced at Lott as he turned them toward his home about a half mile away.

"He's got all the files there are on the first case," Julia said. "And he sounds hungry."

Lott laughed. "Haven't you noticed he's always hungry?"

"This time I think we should have gotten a bigger bucket," Julia said.

Lott indicated the bucket of chicken between them. "I figured as much, so I got the largest one."

"Smart man," she said, laughing.

Damn that chicken smelled good. She was hungry as well. And it was everything she could do to watch the road ahead instead of digging into the bucket.

Everything.

And if the drive had been even a half-mile longer, her self-control would have collapsed.

CHAPTER NINE

LOTT SAT THE large and very warm bucket of KFC on the table and turned to help Julia dig out napkins and paper plates. The wonderful scent from the chicken filled the kitchen like a soft padding, making it feel even more like a home.

He had also gotten some mashed potatoes and some corn for all of them, so he also got out forks.

Julia got them both a bottle of water from the fridge, then poured them both a glass of iced tea as well from a pitcher of tea he had made the day before.

This remodeled kitchen felt wonderful to Lott. It made him feel almost rich with the granite counters and new cabinets and brand new fridge and stove. Carol would have loved what he had done with the place.

They had the table set when Annie came in carrying a small file and headed for the fridge to get a bottle of water. She grabbed a second one and held it up as Andor followed her in the back door.

He took it from her without a word, dropped a large file on the table out of the way of the chicken, and took his normal place with his back to the front door.

Andor had sat in that same chair when Annie was a baby in a high chair and Lott and Carol had first bought this place. Now the kitchen was remodeled, Annie was an adult, Carol was gone, and Julia sat in Carol's spot. All the while Andor remained in his same place and Lott remained in his same chair. Strange how things changed, and yet remained the same in so many ways.

They made small talk about the heat and the smell of the chicken as they dug in and got through their first pieces. For some reason, that first piece of KFC just calmed him down, made him feel like he was on track, no matter what was going on in the world. That response had only happened since Carol's death, and he had no intention of trying to change it or cut back on the chicken.

After finishing the first leg, Lott decided it was time to tell Andor and his daughter about Kirk.

He and Julia explained what Mitchell's home looked like and what she was like, then told them that Kirk was dead.

"Seriously?" Andor asked, stopping halfway through a bite of his second piece of chicken. "Can we be sure of that?"

"He's dead," Annie said, nodding. "Fleet and his people discovered that about two hours ago and double-checked everything. Ruled a suicide. Photos of his body and everything in there if you want to check them out."

She pointed to the folder she had brought, but didn't pull it closer. Lott sure didn't care to look and no one else asked for the file either.

Kirk was just a tragic kid, swept up by a horrible accident. It was amazing he lived as long as he did after the events in the cave and on the bus.

Lott also wasn't surprised that Annie had come up with the same information he and Julia had found. Doc and Fleet and their crew were really amazingly efficient.

"So our one suspect was dead before someone murdered the women we found in the cave," Andor said, shaking his head. "This damn case is something."

Lott had to agree with that.

"The kid has no relatives that we could find in any record," Annie said, "so that side of things is a complete dead-end."

"What about all the abductions?" Julia asked. "Anything coming together from all of them?"

"Fleet and his people are eliminating numbers of the ones we found in the first pass," Annie said.

"That's good," Julia said.

Lott could only agree with that.

"Down to just under two hundred black-haired women who have gone missing over the last seventeen years in the western part of the United States."

Two hundred! That number still felt like a kick in the stomach to Lott. An impossible number of women vanished and families destroyed.

Annie went on. "The only detail that is standing out as slightly similar on a number of missing person's cases is a brown panel van seen near where some of the women were before their disappearances. No license plate was ever taken, or description of any driver."

"And the news just gets better," Andor said, wiping off his hands from the chicken grease. "So why, if Kirk is dead, were you wanting every detail of the school bus tragedy?"

Julia took another piece of chicken and nodded for Lott to tell his former partner his idea.

"The underwear off those girls," Lott said. "I'm betting Kirk claimed he didn't do that."

Andor nodded. "He continuously claimed that, over and over in the records I got here." Andor pointed to the thick file.

"So the eleven abducted women in our mine were not wearing underwear either," Lott said.

"Because the meat on their butts and legs had been trimmed away," Andor said. "But I see where you are going with this. Someone else got into that cave with those girls and Kirk, more than likely before the rescue, but after he was passed out."

"Maybe after the girls were already dead," Lott said. "So do any of those reports from the detectives or doctors have Kirk claiming he had visions of ghosts in that cave?"

"Visions that would have been discounted as heat stroke," Julia said.

"Exactly," Lott said. "And since that was just a massive tragedy with no crime involved, no one would be thinking someone else might have been in there and not reported it at once."

"Never looked for that," Andor said, pulling the file closer and opening it. He quickly divided the large stack of papers into four piles and they all went to reading, trying not to get too much chicken grease on the papers as they went.

Finally, Lott decided he just didn't have the room and stood and picked up the bucket of chicken and moved it to the countertop. He didn't feel like he was finished eating yet, but they could finish later.

Julia and Annie handed him their plates and he took Andor's and dumped them all in the garbage.

Then he sat back down and kept reading, letting the silence fill the kitchen.

"Got it!" Annie said after just a minute. "Kirk told one doctor he was sure he had seen someone in the mine as well. He says the kid gave him a sip of water, said help was on the way, and then left."

"So that's why Kirk survived and the girls didn't," Andor said. "Did Kirk identify the kid?"

Annie shook her head. "Kirk said here he didn't know who it was. The doctors didn't believe Kirk. Chalked it up to the heat since no one came forward and reported being in there."

Suddenly, Lott had a horrid thought. "We need to find out if Kirk went back to the same high school while staying with the Mitchells. And we need to really look at the file on Kirk's death. What time of the day and was he alone?"

"Oh, shit," Andor said. "You think?"

All Lott could do was shrug. "If the guy that took those girl's underwear off suddenly realized Kirk would recognize him, I wouldn't put anything past him."

Annie grabbed the file on Kirk's suicide by bus that had been ignored and opened it.

"Ten at night," she read. "A dark stretch of Tropicana. Bus driver was a woman who said she never even saw Kirk until he was suddenly in front of her bus and she hit him."

Lott watched as Annie read on silently, then shook her head. "No one else was with him, supposedly. And there were no witnesses at all."

"Which means our perp might have been there," Andor said, "and just took care of the only surviving witness to the first panty raid."

"Very possible," Lott said.

And he had a hunch they had just gotten a lead. Not much of one, but a start.

And right about this point, they needed a start.

CHAPTER TEN

JULIA SAT ACROSS the wooden table in Lott's kitchen and watched as Annie called Fleet and Doc in Idaho.

"We need the class list of anyone in the same high school as Kirk. His year and the two years ahead."

"Thanks," she said after a moment. "Kick them through to my computer and Dad's computer. We'll get back to you on some search parameters as we figure it out, but in the meantime, could you also send through if each person from the classes is still alive and what they do for a living and where they live? And also a list of the other girls in the Catholic girl's school where the victims went?"

Again, Julia watched as Annie nodded and then said, "Thanks."

Annie looked at the table. "They are going to also search to see if any of them have a panel van."

Julia was impressed. "Great thinking."

Annie shook her head. "Fleet and Doc are both so upset by all this, they are going at this full tilt. That many women being missing has them both upset beyond anything I have seen in a year or more."

"Not exactly making us all happy," Andor said.

Julia laughed. "Got that right."

The silence filled the kitchen and Julia was about to stand to get the chicken so they could all have more when a thought crossed her mind.

"Black hair," she said.

The other three turned and looked at her.

"How long was that school bus missing?"

"Two days," Lott said, looking at her puzzled. "The file I read had everyone searching for it, but in the wrong area of desert."

Andor nodded. "The governor thought of pulling in the guard to help in the search at one point."

"That's what the newspapers said as well that I read," Annie said. "Headlines for days."

"What about black hair?" Lott asked, looking puzzled.

Julia looked intensely at Annie. "What grade were the girls in?"

"All of them, including Kirk, were sophomores at Saint Mary's School for Girls," Annie said.

"They still had that kind of dress code for kids around here in 1988?" Andor asked.

Julia was surprised at the same thing.

"The girls all went to a small Catholic girl's school," Annie said. "Kirk went to just a regular public school."

"So what's the connection?" Lott asked Julia, his dark eyes trying to see what she was thinking. And at times she was convinced he managed just that.

She smiled. "Black hair. The women in your mine all had black hair. Which one of the girls in that first tragedy had black hair?"

"And did she have a boyfriend?" Andor asked, smiling.

"Exactly," Julia said and watched Lott nod.

"The bus and girls were missing for two days," Annie said. "Everyone in the city would have been out searching for them, and if this ghost that Kirk saw found them first and the girls were dead, including his girlfriend, that would twist any kid up real bad."

Julia nodded to that. "We need to check the file on the first tragedy. How many girls' underwear were found in Kirk's pocket?"

They all quickly went back to the pages on the table in front of them and it was Lott who found the reference first in his part of the report.

"There were ten pairs there," Lott said.

"Eleven girls," Annie said.

"So our killer keeps the women's underwear as trophies," Andor said. "And I'm betting he was in that mine with Kirk."

"Sure looking that way," Julia said. "Now all we have to do is figure out which kid in three classes of high school kids was dating a black-haired Catholic girl who died in the tragedy."

Andor laughed. "No footwork there at all."

"That's what they pay us the big bucks to do," Lott said.

"Yeah, I wish," Andor said, as everyone laughed and Julia got back up to bring the bucket of chicken back to the table with more plates. They still had a dinner to finish.

PART TWO

THE FIRST HAND

CHAPTER ELEVEN

LOTT WAS NOT pleased at all that yet another poker night had come and gone and they hadn't made much progress on the mine murders. It had been one of the longest seven days that he could remember, and he had nightmares every night, sometimes waking up Julia.

She looked tired as well, and he offered to stay at home some night to allow her to get some sleep and all she had said was, "Don't you dare."

It seemed she was having as rough a time with this horrid case as he was.

Over the week, Doc and Fleet had narrowed down the list of missing to about eleven women with black hair per year that had gone missing since 1998. And they had found out the identities of the two unknown women in the mine that the Las Vegas police could never identify.

He and Julia and Annie had spread out all over the entire area, interviewing anyone who might have known the two girls in the mine with black hair. But there were some classmates that were dead, others just had no memory from school in 1988.

Now they were all headed once again after the poker game for the café at the Bellagio Casino, just as they had done a week before.

Over the game, the five attending retired detectives all brain-stormed on various ways to come at this case.

Nothing at all came out of that.

Just more questions.

Why eleven per year?

Why the black hair?

And the question that bothered Lott the most was where were the missing women and why in fifteen years had no others been found?

As the leads with the students seemed to be fading, Doc and Fleet were digging deeper into the mines involved, both the one above the broken down school bus and the one they had found the women in. There was no connection at all between the two mines, but the one with the murdered women seemed to have a somewhat shady past.

Of course, for mines in Nevada, that was not at all unusual. But it was taking time even for Fleet's miracle computer people to dig through the layers of ownership on that mine.

Lott and Julia dropped his car in valet parking and stepped quick-ly through the heat and into the coolness of the casino. The sounds of machines and bells and people laughing and talking seemed almost comfortingly normal as Lott and Julia took their spot in a back booth at the cafe, neither saying a word.

A minute later, Annie joined them, followed by a sweating and red-faced Andor. He had clearly parked out in the lot. Even though it was after ten and the sun had just gone down an hour before, the temperature outside still topped one hundred and twelve degrees.

"I had an idea on the way over here," Andor said as he slid into the booth and took a cloth napkin to wipe the sweat off his face. Then he dipped the napkin in a glass of ice water and put it on his neck.

"So what's the idea?" Lott asked.

"We're going about this wrong," Andor said.

Julia laughed. "No kidding."

"We need to focus on why those women were cut up like they were," Andor said, the red flush in his face slowly fading.

"We are pretty convinced it started in the bus tragedy," Annie said. "But nothing in that tragedy leads to harvesting flesh."

"Exactly," Andor said.

"We think the ghost that Kirk saw in the mine is our perp, right?" Andor asked. "The one that gave Kirk a little water, took off the women's underwear, and then left."

All three of them nodded. Lott had learned a long time ago that when Andor had an idea, it was just better to not say anything and let him run with it.

"So what did our perp learn to do that forces him to cut off the meat from his victims after he roasts them?"

Lott understood where his partner was going. "And how does he bake them?"

"Exactly," Andor said, pointing at Lott as he often did when Lott had something right. "We looked into that some back in the day, but this baking has, in theory, been going on now for another fifteen years. Which one of Kirk's classmates owns either mines or something that could bake a person?"

"Or both," Annie said.

Annie grabbed the phone and a moment later was explaining to Fleet what they wanted. Doc had stayed in Boise to help out and had been calling in favors all over the West investigating some of the women's disappearances to try to get any little detail that would help. So far he had come up empty, but he was still going at it.

The petite brown-haired waitress took their drink order and their food order at the same time just after Annie finished.

"None of the men in Kirk's high school has any interest or family in mining at all," Annie said. "They had already done that search. They are now going after ovens and class members."

"Damn," Andor said. "So why, beyond some strange sexual thing I have never heard of, would a guy cut off a woman's butt and large muscles in her thighs?"

"Steaks, roasts, maybe jerky," Annie said.

"Damn dry steaks and roast," Lott said. "From my little experiment. But jerky makes sense if the flesh was going to be eaten."

"How much was taken from each body?" Julia asked.

"A lot," Andor said. "Maybe twenty pounds or so from each woman if I remember the autopsy reports right."

"That's a lot of jerky every month," Lott said.

"So we let Fleet and his people do the searches and see what they come up with."

Everyone nodded and then sat there silently, just letting the casino sounds wash around them.

Lott felt the frustration of the week climbing back. Just so many odd details and none of it was fitting together. He knew it had to be the mines that were at the center of this in some fashion or another. He just couldn't figure out how.

He turned to Julia. "You up for a trip to visit a couple of mines tomorrow while we wait for Fleet's search to be done?"

"Not really," she said. "But I see where you are going and I think I need to see them as well."

"I'll go with you," Annie said. "I've been feeling that the mines are the key to this all along, just don't know how."

"I'm in," Andor said. "But I'm going to be bringing a cold pack for my neck."

Lott laughed. "Field trip."

"Let's hope it turns out a bunch better than the field trip those girls in the bus took," Andor said.

"We're bringing cases of bottled water," Annie said, "cell phones, and telling Doc and Fleet exactly where we are every hour."

"Where's the adventure in that?" Andor asked, shaking his head.

"Thank you," Julia said, smiling at Annie.

Lott could only smile at his daughter as well and say the same thing.

CHAPTER TWELVE

AUGUST 14TH, 2015
9 A.M.
OUTSIDE OF LAS VEGAS

WHERE THE BUS had gotten lost was surprisingly close to Las Vegas city limits, yet it felt remote and very isolated. But in the intense heat of a summer's day, close was still a death sentence without protection.

Lott took the Cadillac SUV expertly along the narrow dirt road up the rocky canyon. He could only imagine a bus up here in this kind of heat. It was well over a hundred already outside and would be climbing as the day went on.

That kind of heat got very deadly very quickly.

Lott had on a light long-sleeved shirt with the sleeves rolled up and suntan lotion all over his arms, face and neck. He smelled more like a coconut than he liked, but he also didn't spend much more than a few minutes a day in this sun and he wanted to be prepared.

He had also brought a wide-brimmed hat.

They all wore jeans and hiking boots and both Julia and Annie had on tank tops with a light open jacket over that to protect their arms some and wide-brimmed Panama hats.

Andor had on a dress shirt with the sleeves rolled up and a ton of lotion smeared all over his arms and face and neck as well. He had on a baseball cap and a wet towel over his neck that he planned on dipping in iced water from a cooler before he got out.

They had a couple cases of bottled water and some food in the back, plus a cooler full of ice and water bottles. They were about as ready as four detectives without any desert experience could get to go look at some mines in hot desert heat.

Lott decided to come into the canyon from the top of a slight ridge, the same way the bus had gone. From the top of the ridge, it took him only a few minutes going along the winding, one-lane dirt road of the canyon before he found where the bus had broken down.

He pulled the car over and stopped, letting it run and the air conditioning working to keep the inside of the car cool. The car blocked the dirt road completely.

On the left side of the car were steep rock walls. The mine was up a brush-covered slope on the right and still in operation, from what it looked like from the fresh dirt. A rough dirt road twisted up through the brush toward the mine tailings.

No cars or people were in evidence.

Lott was surprised at how far up the hill the mine was from the road.

They had expected that the mine would be in use, but it still sort of surprised Lott. It had actually been in operation when the girls died in there, but the owner had been out of town.

"We need to get a complete background check on the owner of this mine," Andor said.

"Fleet already has it," Annie said, handing Andor the file. "The guy that is working this now is an attorney from Las Vegas, working the mine on weekends. He bought it from the guy who owned it when the girls died. Seemed the guy could never go back into the mine after all the death in there and it took him five years to find a buyer."

"What happened to that guy?" Andor asked a moment before Lott could.

"Died seven years ago," Annie said.

Lott nodded. Figured that would be yet another dead end on a case full of them.

Lott glanced at Julia, then around at Annie and Andor behind him. "Anyone have any desire to walk up there and look around?"

"Not a bit," Andor said. "That's a pretty good hike."

"I can't see a reason to now that I see it from here," Annie said.

Julia nodded. "Carrying those girls up that road must have been almost impossible."

"Especially for two men who had just tried to go for help in heat like this," Annie said.

Silence filled the car.

Lott stared at that road. Impossible described the feat. Kirk and his father could not have done it. Not after trying to go for help and getting turned back by the heat.

Lott swung around and looked at his old partner in the back seat.

Andor was staring up at the mine and frowning.

"You thinking what I'm thinking?" Lott asked.

Andor nodded. "No chance in hell Kirk and his dad carried those eleven girls up that hill. More than likely they got back to the bus after trying to go for help and just passed out with everyone else."

Julia frowned. "So who carried them up there and why?"

"And then why not admit it?" Annie asked.

Lott shook his head. "More questions. No answers."

"This damn case is driving me crazy," Andor said.

Lott and Julia nodded together, both staring up the hill at the mine.

"Let's see the other place, Dad," Annie said. "Maybe we can see something there that will make sense of this."

Lott nodded and with one last look at the mine up on the hillside, he put the car in gear and headed down the dirt road.

About a quarter mile down the winding narrow dirt road, he glanced at Julia. "What in the hell was the bus full of kids doing up here anyway?"

"I didn't see the answer to that in the file," Andor said. "They were supposed to have been up between Boulder City and the dam on the other side of town. That's why it took so long to find them out here, on the north side of town."

"There's a ton more to this tragedy than what is in that record," Annie said.

Lott could only agree with that.

"There sure is," Andor said. "And I think the chief of police can help me get to the bottom of it all this afternoon."

Lott smiled. He knew that tone in his old partner's voice and no way in hell was he going to take no for an answer.

"I'm going to get Fleet and Doc digging as well," Annie said, pulling out her cell phone.

"Good idea," Andor said. "Usually when I smell this much fish, there's an ocean nearby."

Julia and Annie laughed and Lott just smiled and shook his head as he kept working the SUV down the canyon and back toward the city. He had heard Andor use that phrase a bunch over the years. And when he did, there had always been something very wrong about a story.

Always.

And Lott had a hunch, this time would be no exception.

CHAPTER THIRTEEN

JULIA WAS SURPRISED when Lott pulled off the paved highway and headed along a straight dirt road toward some low hills, dust billowing up behind their SUV.

After leaving where the bus tragedy had happened, Lott had wound his way back to Highway 95, gone only about two miles back toward Vegas, and turned off again.

"These two sites are very close together in the scheme of things," Julia said.

"They are at that," Lott said. "We didn't know about the bus tragedy fifteen years ago, so this didn't seem odd."

"It seemed like a long damn ways out in the desert," Andor said.

The dirt road went into a narrow canyon and Lott slowed down, moving up through the curves slowly until the canyon seemed to open up and there, beside the road, was an old mine entrance.

This one had no climb to get to it at all. Hauling bodies from a van or truck or car and getting them into the mine would be easy.

"Well, this brings back nightmares," Andor said.

Lott had stopped the SUV directly across from the mine and was sitting there, just staring at it.

Julia eased her hand over and put it on his leg for support as she too just stared at the mine entrance.

"Boarded up just as we found it," Andor said. "Shit I hate this place."

Julia understood that. She had seen the pictures of what those women in there looked like. She could only imagine finding them.

Lott glanced at Julia. "I think I'll wander over there and chase some demons away."

Julia squeezed his leg and nodded. "I'll go with you."

"You don't need to," Lott said.

"But I do," Andor said as he opened the cooler between him and Annie and dunked in his towel in the ice water, then put it around his neck.

"We'll all go," Annie said. "We're here to look for something, anything, that might give us a clue to move forward."

Lott shut off the car as Julia opened the door and stepped out into the heat. It felt like putting her head in an oven. The air off the dirt and rocks was so hot, it just seemed to radiate from everywhere.

"We can't be out in this too long," Annie said as she got out and moved to the side of the road with Julia.

"Luckily that mine is only about thirty paces off the road," Andor said.

"Think that fact might be important?" Annie asked.

Julia nodded. "It could be."

With Andor walking ahead of them in his normal bullish fashion, Julia followed with Annie and then Lott right behind her. There was a rough path to the mine, but nothing really. More than likely still left from fifteen years ago.

And she knew it was far, far too hot for snakes to be moving around, but she watched the shadows along the path anyway.

The mine opening had been dug between a large rock outcropping. A massive sign was faded, but plastered across the wood covering the mine entrance. It said, "No trespassing. Dangerous Conditions!"

"This is exactly how we found it," Lott said. "Same sign and all."

Julia touched Lott's back for comfort. This had to be almost impossible for him to come back to.

"We were about to not open it and just ignore the psychic," Andor said, "but Mr. Nose here thought he smelled something."

"I still smell it," Lott said. "That memory is so damn strong."

Julia frowned and glanced at Annie, who was also frowning.

"A musty smell, like something had gotten wet in a closed-up garage?" Annie asked.

"Yeah, that's the smell," Lott said.

"I'm smelling it now," Julia said.

"So am I," Annie said.

Lott had a panicked look in his eyes that Julia could never imagine the man she loved having.

"That smell can't still be here," Lott said.

"But it is," Annie said.

Julia watched as both Lott and Andor went at the side of the boards.

They pulled them and the sign off without so much as a grunt. That was not a good sign. That meant this mine had been entered a bunch of times and the boards put back up.

The smell hit them all hard the minute the mine opened up.

Julia just sort of held her ground. She had smelled a lot of smells over the years as a detective, but this one seemed to just clog every pore of her body in the heat.

All four of them pulled out their phones and turned on their lights.

Lott turned to Annie. "Stay out here. One of us has to call for help if this thing collapses."

Julia saw Annie start to protest, then nod.

Lott stepped into the smell of the small tunnel first, followed by Andor.

Julia followed, bracing herself for what she would find just as she had done all the time when on full duty.

The thick overhead wooden beams were low and Lott almost had to duck.

Julia was right behind Andor, but she couldn't see much ahead of them since the tunnel was so narrow.

Ten feet in both men stopped, side-by-side in the narrow tunnel, holding up their lights to illuminate what was in front of them.

Julia moved up and looked between them, gently touching Lott on the shoulder to get him to lean a little out of the way.

Eleven women, dressed in schoolgirl uniforms, were sitting against the mine wall on the left. All had black hair, cut and trimmed exactly the same.

All were mummified completely.

It was the most horrific sight she had ever seen.

Ever.

And with the thick smell of dried death clogging her every sense, she had no doubt that she would ever be the same.

CHAPTER FOURTEEN

LOTT SAT BEHIND the wheel of the SUV, letting the air-conditioning blow directly on his face.

They had managed to talk Annie out of going into the mine after they came out and had just gone back to the car to call for help.

Annie was about to call 911 as they got out of the intense heat and into the car when Andor stopped her. "We need to get the chief out here and only a few detectives he can trust."

Lott had turned to look at his partner as he wiped down his face with the iced towel, then put it back on his neck.

Julia was looking as if she was in complete shock.

"Why?" Annie asked, still holding her phone.

"The last thing we want to do is force this sicko to go to ground at this point," Andor said. "This creep has been thinking he can get away with this for fifteen years. We need him to keep thinking that for just a few more days while we track him down."

"You think we're closer now than an hour ago?" Julia asked.

"I do," Andor said and Lott was starting to understand what Andor was talking about.

"We now will have the entire force back on this case," Lott said. "Combine all those resources with the resources of Fleet and Doc and the four of us and we might stop this guy if we keep this discovery silent for just a day or so."

The car was filled with only the sounds of the blowing air-conditioning. More than anything, he wanted to get home and take a long, long shower to get the smell off, but he knew that wasn't going to be possible for some time now.

Andor started to dial his phone. "I'll get the chief out here. And he's going to have to pull some strings with the State Police as well to keep this under wraps, if he agrees."

Lott nodded. Beside him Julia nodded as well.

She had been supportive of him going into this, now he eased his hand over and touched her leg to offer his support in return.

She smiled and put her hand on his and then nodded that she would be all right.

Lott knew she was one damn tough cop. She would be affected by what she had seen in that mine, but she would be all right in the long run.

"At least we have closed eleven missing persons' cases today," Lott said softly, "and given some families some closure."

Julia nodded and took a deep breath of the cool air pouring over her.

Lott glanced back over at the mine. They had left it open, the boards pulled to one side.

He really wasn't looking up at the mine, just at it across a small distance from the road.

And he suddenly had another idea.

He turned in his seat to look at his daughter as Andor waited for the Las Vegas Chief of Police to come on the phone.

"Can you get Fleet and Doc to search records of abandoned mines in a fifty mile radius of Las Vegas," Lott asked.

"They have already done that," she said. "There are upwards of five hundred."

"Have them sort the mines for elevation to the nearest road," Lott said, pointing over at the mine. "Use this mine as a baseline."

Julia looked at him. "You think our perp doesn't like to carry bodies up hills?"

"That's exactly what I think," Lott said as Annie smiled and pulled out her phone. "I think he did that from that school bus and never wants to do it again."

"I'm going to tell Doc and Fleet what we found," she said, nodding. "I'll tell them we're going to try to keep it under wraps for a day or so."

Lott nodded and about that point Andor got on the line with the chief.

Annie climbed out into the heat and closed the door quickly.

"Chief," Andor said. "The gang has something and it ain't pretty. No announcement to anyone, just grab a few detectives you can trust to keep their mouths shut and a couple of forensic boys and get out here."

Andor nodded. "Chief, just trust me. You need to see this and we need to keep a lid on it for a day or so if we're going to catch this bastard."

Andor nodded at what the chief said, then said. "You know the cold case we are working with the eleven dead women? We're at the same mine. Directions are in the file."

Andor then hung up and nodded to Lott, who had turned and watched him talk to the chief. "He'll be here in thirty minutes without fanfare. He said he'll look at the situation and decide."

At that moment, Annie climbed back in. Just less than a minute in the sun had her sweating.

"Fleet's people are running the mine elevations in relationship to nearby roads now and will text the results to me shortly," Annie said, digging into the cooler for a bottle of water. "Both Doc and Fleet will be on their jet and headed this way in an hour and will be in town in the middle of the afternoon."

"Good," Lott said. "We're going to need as much help as we can get very shortly."

Julia frowned. "Why do you say that?"

Lott pointed over at the mine. "There were eleven women in there. One year's worth if this sicko is doing what we think he's doing."

"It's been fifteen years," Julia said softly.

"Shit," Andor said.

"There are fourteen more mines full of bodies," Julia said, her voice gaining strength with each word.

Lott nodded, trying not to let the image of those eleven mummified women in that mine come back to his mind.

"We need to find those other mines," Lott said, "and then put it all together and stop this. And fast."

CHAPTER FIFTEEN

AUGUST 14TH, 2015
11:30 A.M.
OUTSIDE OF LAS VEGAS

LOTT HAD MOVED the SUV off to a wide area in the dirt road and just down from the mine entrance by the time the three other cars arrived.

All four of them got out of the car, and moving slowly in the intense heat, went back up the road as Chief of Police Dan Beason, a thin man with bright eyes and a disarming smile, climbed out of one of the unmarked cars.

Lott liked the chief more than he wanted to admit.

Chief Beason stood a good six-three and just towered over everyone around him. He had thick, dark-brown hair and had taken off his jacket coat to show he was wearing suspenders with bright red stripes over his blue dress shirt.

Lott had never seen him without a jacket, so the look was startling and seemed to give the chief even more power.

"Detectives," the chief said, nodding to all of them as they walked up along the dirt road. "What's the discovery?"

Andor pointed at the mine. "Fifteen years ago we found eleven women all dressed like school girls in that mine."

The chief nodded and said nothing.

"Our theory," Andor said, "is that the perp has been taking women at eleven per year for the last fifteen years from around the country, baking them, cutting meat off them, and staging them like a class of school girls in mines."

"Shit," the chief said and two other detectives who had come up beside him went pale.

Lott didn't know them other than by reputation. Jones and Schmidt. The top team working at the moment. Lott and Andor used to hold that spot before they had decided to retire to take care of their dying wives.

Andor pointed at the mine. "We came back here today wondering if we could find some clues or see something we had missed the first time around and smelled that same damn sick smell of musty death, so we opened up the mine."

The chief glanced at the open mine only about fifty paces away. "Are you serious?"

"Don't go in there if you want to sleep for the next month," Lott said.

At that, the chief and the two detectives and three others all turned for the mine.

"No point in standing in the sun," Andor said.

They all turned and headed back to the SUV and Lott got it going and the air-conditioning on full.

They all watched in silence as the two detectives went in first, somehow convincing the chief to stay in the sun from the animation of the conversation.

After about two minutes, both came out, shaking their heads and not looking happy.

Two of the other cops went in and less than fifteen seconds later one of them came out, stepped off to the side of the mine entrance, and lost what must have been a pretty good lunch.

Lott remembered doing that himself on his first real death scene with a body that had been rotting in the sun for a few days. Nothing at all compares to that sickly odor of human death.

At that moment the chief just turned and started back toward the road.

"Better move the cooler out of the way and scoot over, Annie," Lott said.

Andor put the cooler over the seat and into the back and, as the chief approached their car, Annie opened the back door and moved over closer to Andor.

The chief crawled in, slammed the door and then let out a huge sigh. "Oh, thank you."

Annie handed him a bottle of cold water and he drank half of it. Then he said, "So you think we can catch this bastard if we hold this information for a day or so?"

Lott had turned around to face where the chief was sitting and Julia had done the same from her seat.

"I do," Lott said. "Doc Hill and his partner, Fleet, have been using all their resources to track missing women with black hair from around the western states. They have found just under two hundred and Doc has all the law enforcement offices in those areas combing the files for clues that we can put together into a large picture."

"Two hundred missing women?" the chief asked, his eyes large.

Lott remembered that feeling as well. A stunning number.

"The guy seems to take them at eleven per year," Andor said. "He was somehow involved in the old bus tragedy near another mine where eleven school girls died when their bus broke down."

"We don't know how, yet," Annie said, "Since the only survivor was killed, a fake suicide we think, about a year after the initial tragedy."

"Shit, just shit," the chief said, shaking his head.

Lott could not have agreed more.

"We think our perp," Andor said, "was the one who carried all the girls from the school bus up to the mine. We think one of the two with black hair in those girls might have been his girlfriend or something like that. We're digging on that now."

The chief nodded. "Glad you have Doc and Fleet with you on all this."

"So are we," Lott said.

"There might even have been more than one who carried those girls out of that bus tragedy," Annie said. "But that's the key to all this, we are convinced."

Lott couldn't imagine how it felt to suddenly have all this information being tossed at the chief, but the guy was smart and was known for making solving crime more important than politics.

"Also a key," Julia said, "is the baking of the women. That takes a pretty large oven and we're searching those, trying to cross-reference anyone from those girl's age who owns an oven large enough to roast a woman without really burning the flesh."

"And what is our perp doing with the large amounts of flesh he cuts from every woman?" Andor asked. "Major question."

"He bakes them and cuts them up?" the chief said, looking startled. "Sorry, I haven't read this old cold case."

Andor nodded. "The perp harvests the meat from the women's butts and legs after he bakes them into what looks like a mummy. He drugs them, but the baking is what kills them."

The chief looked like he might be sick and Lott didn't blame him in the slightest.

Andor went on. "Then he dresses them in school girl costumes, trims their hair all the same exact length, and stages them in a mine just as the eleven girls were in the first bus tragedy, all without underwear."

"When we caught this case back fifteen years ago," Andor said, "we didn't know about that original bus tragedy back in 1988."

"Never put it together until now," Andor said.

The chief just sat there, shaking his head.

At that moment, Annie's cell phone chirped like a lost bird. She glanced at it, then she said, "The mine information is in from Fleet."

She looked at it and then glanced up at Lott. "There are two dozen closed up old mines this close to a road. All are owned by the same company that owns this mine. Fleet and his people are digging at the company, trying to find out who is behind it."

"Where is the closest?" Lott asked, not really wanting the answer, but needing it.

Annie glanced at her phone. "Just over a mile from here."

"Hang on," the chief said, "I'm coming with you."

He opened the door and went back to the detectives cooling off in the cars behind him. Then he returned to their car and got in.

"I got three of them staying here until we decide what to do," the chief said. "Jones and Schmidt are coming with us."

Lott nodded and with a quick motion buckled up his belt and headed the car down the road.

"Give me directions," he said to Annie.

And less than five minutes later they pulled up across from another old, boarded up mine. The mine was similar to the last one, just off the road, with a cliff face on one side of the dirt road and the mine cut into an area between two rock faces.

Lott flat didn't want to know what they would find as all five climbed out into the intense heat. But he had no choice.

They had to look.

Chapter Sixteen

JULIA WALKED BEHIND Lott and the chief of police along a small dirt path toward the mine. Lott was leading and carefully watching the shadows in the brush and rocks for any snakes. There were a certain type of rattlesnake that lived in this kind of area, but the heat would force them down into the rocks.

As they approached the mine, the ground around it cleared of brush and Lott and the chief walked right up to the wood nailed securely over the entrance.

A huge sign the size of the entrance covered the wood warning of no trespassing and danger.

Andor glanced at Schmidt and Jones. "You two want the pleasure."

"Haven't got my stomach back from that last one," Schmidt said.

Andor glanced at Lott and Lott nodded.

They moved up near the mine and both of them shook their heads, then stepped back.

"Same smell," Lott said.

"Damn it," Julia said.

"I'd step back," Andor said. "The first wave out is pretty bad."

The chief and the two active detectives stepped back.

Julia stayed next to Lott until he indicated she should move back as well. "No point in taking this."

She nodded and stepped back next to the chief and Annie about four paces from the mine entrance.

Both Lott and Andor took deep breaths of the hot desert air, stepped to the wood and at the same time, yanked it off.

It came down as easily as the last mine wood had come loose. Clearly it had been taken down and put back up numbers of times.

Both Andor and Lott ducked to one side, coughing.

Then they both clicked on the light on their phones and headed inside.

The chief stepped forward and Julia took his arm. "Trust me, you do not want to see this. The pictures will be bad enough. There is honestly no reason to."

"She's right, Chief," Schmidt said.

"Those two found the original group of women fifteen years ago and have been having nightmares for years about it," Annie said. "You don't need those nightmares."

The chief nodded, but clearly didn't like not going in. Julia liked that about him. Actually, she was liking a lot about the chief in the short time she had known about him and now met him.

She could see Andor and Lott go in about five paces, both of them moving carefully and slowly and ducking to stay under the large timbers that still held the mine up. Then they both stopped, stood there for about ten seconds before turning and coming back out.

Lott looked haunted and wouldn't look at her. "This is one of the oldest ones. Those women have been in there a very long time, I would say over ten years."

"The Cold Poker Gang just solved another eleven missing persons cases," Andor said as he and Lott pocketed their phones.

"Same set-up?" Julia asked, her stomach clamped down into a tight knot.

"Exactly the same," Andor said.

Lott nodded. "Now we got to find the mine that isn't full yet."

The chief looked at him. "Not following you."

"By what Fleet and Doc have found in computer searches of missing persons that match these women's descriptions," Annie said, "Our perp takes women from January through November, one per month from somewhere around eleven western states, taking December off. There have been no missing women in December in the eleven western states that fit this profile in sixteen years."

"So somewhere in this desert we have an old mine with only seven or eight bodies in it," Andor said. "We need to find that mine and get it staked out, which is why we wanted you to keep this all silent."

The chief nodded, his face sweating. Then he turned to look at Annie. "What time of the month do the women normally go missing? Any pattern there?"

"Damn," Annie said, grabbing her phone and hitting a key.

"She's going to find out," Julia said, smiling at the chief. "Great question. One we had not thought of."

The chief turned to the active detectives. "Who else can we trust to not blab their faces off about this?"

"The three at the other mine," Schmidt said. "The rest I wouldn't trust as far as I could toss them to not talk to the press."

The chief nodded. "Get a hammer and then board that mine back up just like it was. Those women will be fine in there for the moment."

Schmidt nodded and turned for his car.

Julia watched as Annie clicked off her phone. "A black-haired woman by the name of Missy Andrews just went missing yesterday from outside of Missoula, Montana. A brown, 1990s panel van was seen close by at one point. No plates or real description."

"So we either get lucky and stop him on the road," Julia said, "or we find where he is baking these women and stop him there."

Lott nodded. "And we do it in the next twenty-four hours to save that woman's life."

Julia just felt her stomach clamp up at that.

"No pressure," Andor said.

"Yeah," the chief said. "No pressure."

CHAPTER SEVENTEEN

LOTT CAME OUT of Julia's shower feeling much better. He had left a number of changes of clothes at her condo at her suggestion, since he often stayed there, and was now glad he did.

He had soaped and scrubbed his skin and hair more than he had done in years to make sure that smell was completely gone. The memory wouldn't leave, but at least the smell would.

He had just finished dressing in jeans and a light blue dress shirt with the sleeves rolled up and was combing his hair when Julia came in. She was wrapped in a towel and her face was red from all the sun.

"I put our clothes in the wash machine," she said. "That might be a smell that will never come out."

He didn't honestly care. He might throw those clothes away even if the smell came out. Anything he could do to not remind himself of seeing that much death in one day would be a good thing.

She turned on the shower, checked the temperature, and then dropped the towel and climbed in while Lott watched.

In his opinion, she was one of the most beautiful women he had ever known. And if they hadn't just spent the day finding more dead bodies than he wanted to think about, he might have offered to scrub her back right at that moment.

But he had a hunch she was as focused on this case as much as he was. And on saving that one woman they knew was headed in this direction and to a certain horrible death if they couldn't stop it.

"I'll be in the kitchen getting a snack," Lott said to the showering woman.

"I won't be long," she half-shouted back.

He headed out of the bathroom, feeling almost human again.

The plan was that they would head for the Café Belagio after showering and getting changed to meet Doc and Fleet and Annie and Andor and plan what to do next.

In the last four hours, they had found all but one of the mines with women's bodies. Schmidt and Jones had taken some of the mine locations, the chief and the other two detectives had taken part of the list. Lott and Julia and Annie and Andor had stayed in Lott's car and taken another third of the list Annie had gotten from Fleet.

The four of them had found three more mines full of bodies.

It had been the chief and the detectives riding with him that had found the one only half full to the south and east of the city.

The chief had set up very discrete watching posts on both entrances to that canyon, hidden completely from view. No way that killer would get out of that canyon if he went in there.

The chief was also going to get officers in the State Police working the highways coming down from the north, watching for any sign of a brown panel van.

And his men were stationed, without knowing why, at all the major entrances to the city watching for the same thing.

And he had promised that nothing would be broadcast at all over any police channel.

Lott got into clean jeans, a long-sleeved white dress shirt, and put on new tennis shoes. More than likely after that smell, he was going to have to toss his favorite tennis shoes.

While he waited for Julia, he took out his small notebook and pen and sat down at her kitchen table overlooking the trees and lawn and pool common area below and started to write a list of things they didn't know yet.

First, what was the connection between the original bus tragedy and the perp? There was no doubt in his mind there was a connection, but they hadn't been able to find it yet.

Second were the unknown factors all the victims had in common besides black hair. He had a hunch there was more. There had to be.

Third, the question of the ownership of the mines. Did someone in that company have anything to do with this? And if so, who?

Fourth, where were the victims taken and how were they baked to death?

Fifth, why were the victim's harvested for meat? Where did cannibalism come into play in this? Or was it even cannibalism? Was the women's flesh being used for something else?

He stared at his list, his eye continuing to go back to the first question. The real key to locating this sick killer was that bus tragedy. If it really was a tragedy and not done on purpose. Why had that bus been so far away from where it had planned on going?

Julia came in while he was staring at the list and wrapped her arms around him and put her chin on his shoulder. She smelled wonderful, with a slight peach scent from the shampoo she used. She had on a light green blouse with a sports bra and jeans and new tennis shoes as well.

"Am I missing anything?" he asked, showing her the list he had been making.

"Underwear," she said. "And why did Kirk need to be killed?"

He wrote both down, nodding.

"A lot of questions, that's for sure," he said.

"Let's hope we don't have to answer them before this sicko is in custody," Julia said as Lott stood.

He looked at her as she stepped away and he stood, putting his notebook back in his pocket. "You think that has a chance of happening?"

"Not a chance in hell," she said, shaking her head. "The person who has been doing this without getting caught for over fifteen years isn't going to be pulled over in a standard traffic stop."

"You think the brown panel van is stored up north somewhere?"

"Of course it is," Julia said. "No chance a van that might be linked to an abduction is going to be driven right to this guy's home and parked."

"I was thinking the same thing," Lott said as they headed out and Julia locked the door behind her.

"So it's up to us to save that woman's life," Julia said. "Because by the time the killer takes her to the mine and gets caught that way, she will be very, very dead."

"The chief can't sit on this long enough for even that to happen," Lott said as they headed down the stairs. "There are a lot of crime scenes in that desert at the moment and he doesn't dare hold this down for more than twenty-four hours. Even that long might cost him his job."

"And when all that hits the papers," Julia said. "We lose our latest victim and any chance of finding this creep."

Lott knew she was right.

They had to crack this case and crack it quick. Time was not on their side.

Or the side of that poor woman from Missoula.

Chapter Eighteen

LOTT AND JULIA didn't talk much as it took a while for Lott to get them through rush hour traffic and to the valet parking at the Bellagio. The heat on the few steps from the car into the casino seemed even worse than normal. More than likely that was because they had been in and out of it all day.

"We're going to need more water," Julia said as they got inside.

Lott nodded. "Felt that."

He let her lead the way toward the café, winding between people and families ambling down the wide tile hallways.

The sounds of the casino wrapped around her and calmed her some. She loved all the people enjoying the machines and the gaming tables and just having wonderful vacations. She seemed to take energy from just being in a casino. It was why she enjoyed the poker tournaments around town at times and coming here for lunches and dinners.

Plus the food was good, with lots of choices, and the staff was always friendly.

Doc, Fleet, and Annie had already secured a round table tucked off in a back corner surrounded on three sides by tall plants and flowers. Almost like a private office right in the middle of the casino.

Julia hugged both Doc and Fleet. Fleet was rail thin and tall, with a slight pot belly. He always wore a silk vest and suit and tonight was no exception, the gray silk making him look dashing and rich. He had lost the tie, something she very seldom had seen him without.

Doc wore jeans and a light dress shirt with the sleeves rolled up, just as Lott often did. Doc was about six feet tall and as solid muscle as a human being could get. He was also about as tan as they came and had just spent most of June and July guiding rafts on the rivers of central Idaho. He had only come out a week before and planned on going back into the River of No Return in three days.

He and Annie made a stunning couple, right off a magazine cover.

Julia had no doubt that if this case was still active in three days, Doc would not be leaving it for Idaho rafting. He took the work he did with Fleet helping the FBI and other police networks very seriously.

Doc and Fleet and Annie always worked behind the scenes, but so far their team had really been instrumental in solving some major crimes. It seems Doc and Fleet had friends in just about every area of police and federal governments, all the way up to the President of the United States.

Julia was constantly impressed by what they could do, all the while seeming to enjoy life and play poker. And, on top of that, Fleet was raising a family of two kids in Boise.

A couple minutes later, Andor came in, leading Chief Beason. Andor was sweating, but both of them had changed clothes and the chief wore jeans, a UNLV tee-shirt, and a baseball cap. No one would recognize him, Julia was sure.

She was surprised that the chief had come along. He clearly felt this group was the best chance at catching this killer.

Doc and Fleet both stood.

"Great seeing you again, Chief," Doc said, shaking the chief's hand.

It was clear to Julia that Doc and the chief liked and respected each other.

"We really appreciate the work you and the gang here have done to break this ugly mess open," the chief said, pulling up a chair with his back to the room.

"We're not done yet," Fleet said.

Everyone nodded to that.

After a moment of small talk about Doc and Annie's summer on the rivers in Idaho, it was Doc who turned the topic back to the case. Julia was always impressed by Doc and now was no exception.

"So where do we stand?"

The chief quickly outlined what he was doing and how long he could hold this silence before all hell broke loose.

"Maybe thirty hours at most," the chief said. "I have two friendly reporters from local stations and one from the Sun Times coming in tomorrow night, after the late news and press time on the paper, to talk with me. I'll have to give them the full story that we have at that point. They won't be able to hold it."

Julia felt her stomach twist and she forced herself to take a drink of water. That was not a lot of time to catch a serial killer who had been working and killing women for over fifteen years.

"You going to be able to handle that many bodies and crime scenes?" Lott asked.

"I have help coming in already from California, Reno, and Salt Lake," the chief said. "I'm talking with the FBI tomorrow afternoon, since this is all across state lines. And at that point I'm going to have to bring in the State Police, since most of this is in their area. But they can't even begin to handle it any more than we can. Between the three agencies and outside help, we'll deal with it."

"I'll give you a list of the women we think are victims," Fleet said, "to contact their families when the time is right to get DNA samples to match."

"Thanks," the chief said. And then he turned and looked directly at Lott, Andor, and Julia. "And thanks to you three for being willing to dig at this. If nothing else, we'll stop this and save some lives."

Julia just nodded, as did Lott and Andor. She felt slightly embarrassed. Detectives were not used to being thanked for doing their jobs. Even if they were retired and still doing their jobs for free.

CHAPTER NINETEEN

THEY HAD ORDERED and the waitress had just turned away when Lott decided it was time to get things organized. He was feeling the time pressure more than he wanted to admit. "I made a list of what Julia and I think are the major questions we are facing that might get to this sicko."

"You don't think our surveillance on the roads will catch this guy?" the chief asked.

Lott shook his head. "It needs to be done, but this guy isn't going to be that stupid. I'm betting that panel van is in a storage unit somewhere in Idaho or Utah or Northern Nevada."

Lott was worried the chief would be angry, but instead the chief just nodded, as did everyone else at the table.

"And once this breaks," Andor said, "the guy is going nowhere near that mine or any mine in this area."

Again everyone nodded.

"So I got six areas of questions," Lott said. "Let me skip the first one because I think it holds the key and see if we can cover these other five and add in what we are missing before going back to number one."

"The bus tragedy number one?" Andor asked.

Lott nodded.

"First," Lott said, turning to look at Fleet and Doc, "besides the black hair, is there anything at all these victims have in common?"

Fleet shrugged. "All normal. Almost without an exception, they had decent jobs of one level or another. Nothing common between the jobs or financial status at all. About half were married or separated. A quarter of them had children, some raising the kids as single mothers. All were between the ages of twenty-two and thirty. And a large percentage of them were outwardly gay. Numbers of them were married to their partners."

"Gay?" Andor asked, sitting forward.

Lott felt the same thing as clearly did the chief, since they both sat forward as well.

"Were these women forcibly abducted, or did they just disappear?" the chief asked.

"They all seemed to have just disappeared," Fleet said. "Almost all had gone out for the night, some with friends, some on their own. They just never returned. It sometimes took a full day or two before someone would report them missing."

Lott made himself take a deep breath and just try to think.

"So how did we get this last report on the Montana woman so fast?" Andor asked.

"The woman only went for some groceries around nine in the evening and was due back within thirty minutes," Fleet said. "When she didn't return, her partner tried to reach her and the victim's cell phone had been shut off. The woman's car was still in the store parking lot with a flat tire."

"No security cams?" Julia asked.

"Nothing in that area of the parking lot," Fleet said. "But through other cams in the area we got a brown panel van leaving the neighborhood right after the abduction."

"So our killer offered to help her with her tire problem," Andor said.

Lott was staring at Julia, who was looking stunned.

"Who would you trust in a parking lot at nine in the evening that you didn't know?" Lott asked Julia.

"Another woman," Julia said softly.

"Damn it all to hell," Andor said. "We've been assuming this was a guy all this time."

"I have a hunch we were wrong," Lott said, feeling as stunned as everyone at the table felt.

Then Fleet pulled out an iPad and clicked up a file as the silence of the table let the casino sounds of laughter and bells ringing flood back over them.

Then Fleet turned the iPad around to show everyone a picture of a middle-aged attractive woman posing for what was clearly a professional picture. She had long blonde hair pulled back off her face and wore a silk business jacket and an expensive blouse in the picture. To Lott, the woman's dark eyes looked dead and piercing.

"Who is that?" Julia asked a half second before Lott got the same question out of his mouth.

"Her name is Karen West," Fleet said. "She is the CEO and President of Roso Industries Inc., a major investment holding company based here in Las Vegas with upwards of forty different corporations under the umbrella. She has a lot of money."

"Let me guess," Lott said. "One of those corporations owns all the mines."

Fleet just nodded.

"I've met that woman a number of times at fundraisers for different charity events," the chief said. "Are you thinking she might be the killer here?"

"Let's find out where she is right now," Lott said. "I would call her a person of interest at the moment."

The chief nodded.

Lott wasn't sure if she was anything more than a person of interest. So far everything about this case twisted into dead ends. More than likely this would as well.

Fleet flipped the screen around, then grabbed his phone.

"Find out where she went to school as well, would you?" Lott asked Fleet, who nodded.

"Any bets?" Andor asked.

"No bet," Lott said. "But if she is the one, the question then becomes that with her money, how do we pin it on her and make it stick? We have no concrete evidence at all, remember?"

"And how do we save the woman she has with her now?" Julia asked.

Lott just nodded.

Damn he hoped this hunch was the right one. He was tired of going back to square one on this case.

PART THREE

PLAYING THE HAND
THAT IS DEALT

CHAPTER TWENTY

AUGUST 14TH, 2015
6:30 P.M.
LAS VEGAS

THEY HAD QUICKLY worked their way through Lott's list, spotting nothing else that made sense. Before they could get back to the bus tragedy, the food started arriving. They were all almost finished with their salads and soup when Fleet got the reply from his people.

Julia had been working on a wonderful hazelnut-dressing dinner salad with extra tomatoes. Even though it tasted wonderful and she knew she was hungry, she was having to force herself to eat. She had no idea how long she would be awake tonight, and she knew she needed to eat and drink water to make sure she was fully recovered from the time in the sun and heat this afternoon.

"Karen West took a week of personal time this last week," Fleet said after hanging up his phone. "She does that most every month it seems. I have my people trying to track down what sort of vehicle she is driving, but my sources tell me she talks to no one about what she does during that week every month."

"That's pretty damning," Andor said, shaking his head.

Julia could only agree with that. Not proof by a long ways, but damning. And one thing detectives tended to know was when all arrows pointed in a certain direction, chances are that direction was the right way. And right now a lot of arrows were starting to turn and point to Karen West.

"She also went to the same Catholic girl's school and was the same age as the girls on that bus," Fleet said, his voice low against the sounds of the casino around them.

He again pulled up an image on his laptop and turned it for everyone to see.

It was clear to Julia it was a young version of Karen West, dressed in the same uniforms as all the women found dead in the mines.

The final arrow.

Julia had no doubt at all now who had killed all the women.

"I think she just moved from a person of interest to the major suspect," the chief said. "I'll get everyone looking for any of her registered cars, or her company's registered cars, coming into town, see if we can spot her that way."

"If we don't catch her in the act, how do we prove she is the killer, assuming she is the killer?" Annie asked. "I'm betting anything these crime scenes in the mines are as clean as the first one Dad and Andor found."

Julia had to agree.

Everyone sat silently, thinking. With a woman of that kind of power and money, that was going to be very difficult at best, unless she had made a major mistake and Julia doubted this Karen West had done that.

"So what the hell happened in that bus tragedy?" the chief asked, breaking the silence.

Julia and Lott quickly went over all the details of the tragedy for the chief as their main meals arrived. She was having a filet of cod, sautéed in butter. Asparagus spears filled the plate, also sautéed lightly in butter.

She worked at it slowly, letting herself savor the taste as everyone got on the same page with the bus tragedy, including their suspicions that it had not been a complete accident.

"So you think this Karen West was the ghost in the mine?" the chief asked. "And carried all those girls up to the mine herself?"

"Not possible," Julia said, and beside her Lott nodded. "She had to have help."

"I'm betting it went down like this," Lott said. "Karen West and a friend somehow managed to give the driver bad directions as a prank, change the destination. I don't think they ever figured the bus to break down. More than likely they were doing it to annoy the teacher."

"I agree," Julia said. "I think the driver and his son, Kirk, went to try to find help, but the father collapsed and died and Kirk turned back to the bus, where he passed out with the girls."

"Then," Andor said, "after the bus had been missing for a day or so, West and her friend decided that was enough and went to where they knew the bus had gone. There they found the teacher dead and most of the girls and Kirk almost dead. They got the girls up to the mine, took most of the panties off all the girls and stuffed them in Kirk's pocket to focus the attention on him, and went to try to let someone know without revealing they were at fault."

"They didn't get the word out quick enough and the girls died," Julia said.

"That had to mess them up something awful," Andor said.

Julia agreed with that completely.

Fleet picked his phone back up, ignoring the half-eaten prime rib in front of him.

The table went silent, listening to his side of the conversation.

"Find out who was Karen West's best friend in school the year of the bus tragedy," Fleet said. "And see if she is still alive or not."

He nodded and then hung up.

They all went back to eating and Julia forced herself to pay attention to the wonderful, light fish on her plate and enjoy the taste. She had a hunch things were going to get really stressed and harried before this was all over.

A moment later Fleet's phone buzzed and he answered it. He listened and nodded as everyone at the table watched him. Then he said, "Thanks," and hung up.

"Her girlfriend's name was Bettie Lynch," Fleet said. "She and Karen West were married a few months back in California."

Suddenly Julia wished she hadn't just eaten that dinner. Her chest and stomach had clamped up so tight, she could hardly breathe.

Around the table the rest of the group sat silent. Some had their forks over their meal, frozen in mid-air. Fleet was looking puzzled at that response.

Finally it was Doc who broke the silence. "Mind telling those of us from Idaho why that was so shocking?"

"Bettie Lynch is a well-known figure here in Las Vegas," Lott said, calmly pushing his plate away.

Julia forced herself to take a deep breath and focus on being calm.

"Lynch has a chain of stores," Andor said.

Suddenly Doc's very tanned face went completely white. "Are you talking about Lynch's Jerky and Treats?"

"The same," Lott nodded.

The chief of police sat there for a moment in the silence, then pulled out his cell phone and called his office. He ordered an emergency meeting in thirty minutes. "Everyone. Get them out of bed."

Then he stood. "We may not have enough evidence to convict, but we're going to get some court orders and search a house and close down some stores. What do I owe for dinner?"

Doc waved him off. "Just catch those two."

"Oh, we will," the chief said. "And first thing we are going to do is test some of the products in those shops."

Julia watched the very angry chief of police storm off through the casino. Then she turned back to the silent group.

"So who thinks he's going to get West and her partner?" Julia asked.

"I wouldn't put money on it," Doc said. "Even though he and other major agencies are going to do their best."

Lott and Andor both nodded.

"So it's up to us. What do we do first?" Julia asked.

"Tomorrow morning at sunrise," Fleet said, "we check to see if that last mine was being watched."

"Because if it was," Doc said, nodding, "those two killers are going to be nowhere near Las Vegas."

Julia agreed.

Now, somehow, after all this today, she needed to get a few hours sleep. She doubted that was going to be possible.

CHAPTER TWENTY-ONE

AUGUST 15TH, 2015
5:15 A.M.
LAS VEGAS

ANDOR HEADED TO the police headquarters while Julia, Annie, Doc, and Fleet came with Lott in his SUV to the last mine, the mine only half-full of bodies. The sun wasn't up over the east hills yet and the air still felt warm, meaning the day would be another hot one.

Julia sat in the front seat beside him as he took the SUV up the narrow dirt road to the east of the city, working carefully along rocks. He loved having her beside him. It just felt right.

Annie, Doc, and Fleet were in the back seat, with Annie in the middle.

"Snakes will be out this time of the day," Doc said.

Annie punched him with her elbow in the ribs.

"I do not plan on leaving the road," Fleet said.

Julia glanced back. "Some snake issues?"

"No issue," Fleet said, his voice very serious. "I hate them, fear them, and will not go near them, so there is no issue."

Lott laughed, as did Doc.

Julia just shook her head, smiling.

Lott stopped the SUV in the middle of the narrow dirt road beside a mine entrance about a hundred paces to the right just slightly up a slight gully. The mine opening in the dark morning shadows looked old and abandoned and had a large sign on it warning no trespassing and danger.

If they had to move up that gulley to that mine, there was no doubt there would be snakes this time of the morning.

They all sat there staring at the boarded up mine, knowing there were women in there who had met a very sudden and horrid death. Lott didn't want to think about it. All he could think about was stopping these two crazy killers and saving that last woman from Montana.

"Stay put for a moment, everyone," Lott said.

He climbed out into the shadows and warm air of the early morning and held his badge up in the air for the cop watching the mine to see. He had no idea where the cop watching this mine was stationed, but he didn't want to take a chance.

"Up here, Detective Lott," a voice said. "I got the heads-up you were coming."

Lott turned to look up through some rocks as a man in a light jacket stood and waved. He had to be a good hundred paces up through the rocks. No chance the guy could have been seen up there if West and her partner had come here.

Lott could only imagine how hot it got up there during the prime of the day.

"We're here to see if this thing was bugged," Lott said.

"Anything I can do, just shout," the cop said.

"Thanks!" Lott said. "The way things are moving, I doubt you'll be here much longer."

"Good to hear," the cop said.

Lott turned and nodded that the rest could get out.

Annie and Julia got out and waved to the cop on the hill.

Doc moved around and opened up the back of the SUV.

Fleet climbed out slowly, looking around before moving to the back of the SUV with Doc and opening up some equipment.

It didn't take him long studying a hand-held device that looked more like an early version of a heavy cell phone before he nodded.

He turned slowly, nodding.

Then he handed another device just like it to Doc. "Go up the road about twenty paces and aim that at the hill above the mine. I'll triangulate the location."

"Is there something here?" Julia asked.

Fleet nodded as Doc headed back up the dirt road twenty paces, then turned and aimed the device at the rocks and dried brush above the mine.

"Twenty paces above the mine and to the right in those rocks," Fleet said, pointing. "There's a camera broadcasting a signal on two minute intervals."

Lott could see exactly where he was pointing. From that spot, the camera could see both the road and the opening of the mine. Lynch and West had watched everything yesterday.

"Can the signal be traced?" Annie asked.

Fleet shook his head.

"So the two women know they have been found," Annie said, her voice low and angry as Fleet motioned for Doc to come back down the road to join them.

"They know," Lott said. "And more than likely they have a very good plan on what to do next."

He was angry, more angry than he wanted to admit even to himself. And now he had no idea how they could ever save that woman from Montana, let alone even find the two women who had killed so many. The two killers had money, they were smart, and they had a head start.

Even with every federal, state, and local law enforcement officer in the western part of the United States looking for them, Lott had no doubt they wouldn't be spotted.

Fleet put the two devices back in a silver case and shut it.

Silently, they all got back into the SUV.

Lott headed the big Cadillac back toward Las Vegas.

"Now what?" Annie said as Fleet dialed the chief of police's number to tell him the bad news.

Not a one of them had an answer.

CHAPTER TWENTY-TWO

AUGUST 15TH, 2015
7:00 A.M.
LAS VEGAS

AS IF THEY all needed comfort food, they headed back to what was turning out to be their meeting headquarters, the café at the Bellagio. Julia rode in silence in the front seat, just doing her best to figure out what to do next.

Annie had called Andor and told him to meet them.

Then, until they reached the area near Las Vegas Boulevard, they continued to ride in silence. Julia could feel the pressure of the anger and the feelings in the car, compounded by the frustration. This group, including her, were not used to having someone beat them.

And at the moment, Lynch and West appeared to have beaten them.

"This is going to explode over every television station and news source in just an hour or so," Annie said. "No point in Chief Beason trying to keep it under wraps now. They might be able to hold most information until later in the afternoon. But no doubt it will be a national firestorm that's going to descend on this city."

"The chief will keep us out of it," Lott said.

"I got my people tracing all of the two women's assets," Fleet said. "Second homes and so on."

"Not worried about us being involved in the media side," Annie said. "I just have no idea how those two women could even think of going underground with this kind of press and manhunt that will happen."

"Let alone with us, and every federal agency," Lott said, "being able to track their every asset and move."

Julia looked at Lott, who was pulling them into the valet parking area of the Bellagio near the café entrance. Around them dozens of cars sat waiting to either be put away or picked up by their owners. All were modern cars like Lott's Cadillac. No telling how many of them were rentals.

A hint of an idea was forming and she let it.

Around her, all the people moved in their own worlds, some with luggage, some just going into the casino. All handing cash to the attendants as a tip to take care of their cars or a thank-you for helping with luggage.

Cash.

Massive numbers of people.

Julia suddenly knew exactly how these two women would escape notice and capture.

Exactly.

Lott put the SUV in park as Julia smiled. "I know how I would escape this in Lynch and West's positions."

Lott's head snapped around to look at her, his wonderful green eyes looking intent.

"I need some real breakfast, though," she said, smiling at him and climbing out of the car.

From the back, Annie laughed.

"Now that's just mean," Doc said, laughing.

They all headed through the warming air into the air condition-ing of the Bellagio and to the café. As Julia watched, Lott slipped the attendant a five-dollar bill to take care of the car.

Julia nodded, letting the idea form even more.

Their regular booth was open in the back, so she waited until they were all seated and the hostess had left and then just smiled. "Lynch and West aren't going anywhere."

Lott just shook his head. "West was already out of town."

"She'll come back here," Julia said, becoming more and more sure of her theory the more she thought about it.

"So what do you think West is going to do with the woman from Montana?" Annie asked.

Beside Annie, both Doc and Fleet were looking at Julia intently.

Julia just shrugged. "I honestly don't know. My hope is that West will give the poor woman a little extra drugs, park her in a hotel room, and be long gone before the poor woman wakes up."

"I hope so as well," Lott said. "But I'm not so sure."

"It sounds logical," Julia said, trying to sound more positive than she actually was.

Annie was nodding, but frowning.

"These women only kill inside one carefully arranged meth-od," Julia said, "that patterns what happened to them with their friends in school. We can hope they won't hurt a woman outside of that pattern."

"Let's just hope like hell they don't have the pattern set up somewhere else," Lott said.

That caused silence and nods from everyone.

"So why do you think they would come back here?" Doc asked.

"This is their home," Julia said.

"They have no other homes or property in this city or even close," Fleet said. "Under any name or corporation cover that is linked to them."

"They don't need a home or anything else," Julia said. She pointed around the casino and then up trying to indicate the massive hotel that rose above them. "They just need new looks, some basic fake id, and cash."

Lott nodded, reaching over and taking Julia's hand. "They're here. You're right."

"I know I'm right," Julia said. "But now how do we find them? And even if we can't convict them, we can put them under wraps and stop more deaths."

And with that, the sounds of the casino and the early morning restaurant washed back in over them, filling the silence at the table.

And outside the restaurant, a steady stream of tourists poured into the building.

CHAPTER TWENTY-THREE

AUGUST 15TH, 2015
7:00 A.M.
LAS VEGAS

LOTT SCOOTED OVER closer to Julia in the booth as Andor joined them a minute before the waitress came back to take their breakfast order.

"It's a flat madhouse at headquarters right now," Andor said. "FBI, state, and a dozen other police forces from around the area are meeting with the chief. So damn crowded, everyone is shouting to just have the person next to them hear what they are saying."

Lott shuddered. He had only seen headquarters like that once before and he never wanted to be there again when that happened.

"What about the bodies?" Julia asked.

Lott nodded. That was his first thought as well.

"They have men guarding at all sites now, mostly to keep the press away. They are waiting for help from Los Angeles and the FBI before they start taking out the bodies and processing the scenes. They are going to set up a refrigerated warehouse near headquarters for a morgue for the bodies."

Lott didn't even want to imagine what that morgue would look like with so many bodies.

"What about the families?" Annie asked.

"The families are going to be staying at different downtown hotels and I think they have one ballroom in one hotel for only family and another ballroom in another hotel for the press. They won't start being notified until later, though."

Lott was impressed. In just a couple of hours the entire mess was being organized.

"The jerky shops?" Doc asked.

"Shut down, and teams are searching Lynch and West's home and offices and other properties," Andor said.

Doc nodded and Lott was very glad at that moment he had never developed a habit of eating jerky. He just hoped that human jerky could be found because that would tie the two women into the murders solidly and be the evidence they needed.

"So what do we have going on here?" Andor asked, glancing around. "Not a soul at headquarters is going to be thinking of how to capture Lynch and West. Too damn busy trying to wrestle this monster we dumped on them. They are going to leave the capture part up to the FBI and even the FBI is too damn busy with this many bodies."

"Julia thinks Lynch and West will come back here," Lott said. "And I agree."

Andor looked puzzled. "Why would they do that?"

"This is a city of cash," Julia said.

"Impossible to trace and not unusual," Fleet said.

"And thousands and thousands of nice suites," Doc said, nodding.

"So you think they are going to hide right here in plain sight?" Andor asked.

"I do," Julia said. "Change their hair color, get fake IDs, have a lot of cash in bank accounts under various false names, and stay at nice suites. They have had a long time to set it up, so I am sure they are very, very prepared."

Lott could only agree with that as well. The more he thought about Julia's idea, the more he liked it. But something about it seemed wrong and damned if he could put his finger on it.

"So any ideas how West got back into town?" Andor asked after the waitress brought the first parts of their breakfasts.

Lott had ordered two eggs, a waffle, and some bacon, which smelled wonderful. Not at all his normal breakfast of cereal and coffee, but this morning was far from a normal morning.

"Just as I am sure the panel van is in a storage locker somewhere up north," Lott said, "I'm betting they had other cars that they had bought with cash and registered under a fake name and had stored in various places along West's normal routes."

Andor and Julia both nodded.

"So it would be easy for them to get back here, and no one would expect them to return," Doc said, nodding. "Logical play. And damn near impossible to find and trace."

"And since Lynch and West had a day's notice that the mine had been found," Annie said, "more than enough time."

Lott hated the idea that the two killers were more than likely holed up in a nice room watching the firestorm break over the news. Maybe in this very hotel.

But Lott had no idea at all how to find them. Las Vegas was a huge city and the two women could look so different, without major facial recognition software, they would never be recognized.

Then suddenly Lott realized what he had been thinking.

He turned to Doc and Fleet. "The security systems of these casinos have facial recognition, don't they?"

"They do," Doc said, smiling. "It's not perfect and it can be fooled, but it will see through an easy disguise."

Beside him Annie was almost bouncing.

"We need to get access to the casino's security systems," Fleet said, grabbing his phone.

Lott didn't want to know how Fleet planned to do that. Casino security systems were more protected than any bank by a long, long ways.

"Would Lynch and West be that stupid?" Julia asked. "They would know about that software as well."

"It's worth a shot," Doc said. "A fake nose or a change in eyebrows and cheek bones made to look higher would fool the system. But still worth the shot."

"It is," Lott said. Then before Fleet could start talking, Lott said to Fleet. "Set the search to find women of Lynch's and West's age who can't be recognized due to one factor or another."

Fleet nodded and turned slightly to give instructions to his computer people while Lott dug into his waffle.

Maybe, just maybe, they might get lucky.

He doubted it would be that easy. And so far, they hadn't caught much of a break on this case.

Luck was going to have nothing to do with capturing those two murdering women. It was going to take some skill and planning and a bunch of work, of that he had no doubt.

PART FOUR

ALL-IN CALL

CHAPTER TWENTY-FOUR

AUGUST 15TH, 2015
9:00 A.M.
LAS VEGAS

EVEN THOUGH THEY had just had breakfast, Lott and Julia stopped for a bucket of KFC on the way back to Lott's home. The plan was to go down to the poker room and watch the television coverage break. The two of them just couldn't think of anything else to do at the moment.

And for Lott, feeling helpless and useless was something he didn't much like at all.

Doc and Annie and Fleet had all headed off to their Las Vegas corporate office to help coordinate the casino's facial recognition search. Doc and Fleet were pulling in a lot of favors to have the casinos do this for them, but at this moment, every casino in town was all on the same side.

Finding this many kidnapped dead women around the town was bad for business and this needed to be put to rest quickly.

Very quickly. Because it was very, very bad for tourism.

Andor had headed back for headquarters, to, as he said, "stick his nose into places it didn't belong."

Lott had no doubt that if anyone in that madhouse could come up with information, it would be Andor.

Lott poured him and Julia a glass of iced tea and they headed downstairs, leaving the bucket of chicken in the fridge.

The custom-made poker table sat to the left of the stairs with a five-bulb light fixture made of wood over it. When that fixture was on, even the oldest of eyes could see cards clearly and read old police files.

A polished oak bar ran down the left wall with black-and-white pictures of old poker masters on the wall behind it, plus a few stacks of different types of glasses and a row of bottles of premium bourbon, scotch, and liquor, most of which had never been opened.

The bar looked impressive, but most of the Cold Poker Gang didn't drink that much, if at all. Lott figured it was too many years on the force watching what booze did to people sort of cut the enjoyment.

Five file folders of varied colors sat on one end of the bar. Those were the cold cases the gang hadn't figured out a way to close yet. Lott sure hoped this ugly mess wouldn't end up on the end of the bar.

A large leather couch filled the wall beyond the bar and two large recliners on either side of it, with an oak coffee table that matched the bar in front of the couch. A large screen television with complete surround sound filled the right wall facing the couch.

Lott flat loved this room, more than any room in the house. It felt totally comfortable and was all his. He had brought nothing of his wife Carol down here. He was so glad that Annie had pushed him to remodel this basement into this wonderful space.

And not only had the Cold Poker Gang met down here for the last couple of years, but Lott and Julia had spent many a wonderful evening on the couch watching movies.

Lott turned on the television to a local channel and a woman news reporter looking young and slightly panicked was talking, going on about a massive breaking murder story.

Lott glanced at his watch. It surprised him when he realized it was still only a little after nine in the morning. It had already seemed like a long day. No wonder the woman on the screen looked panicked. She wasn't the main news anchor.

He and Julia sat on the couch, sipping iced tea and listening until the woman started to repeat herself. Then Lott muted the television sound.

"Nothing until a press conference at one in the afternoon," Julia said, nodding. "Makes sense. The chief and the other agencies need to get this all under control before they brief the public."

Lott could only nod.

They sat there in silence for a short time, both half-staring at the "Breaking News" banner over the poor young announcer's head. He didn't envy the chief's job of trying to explain what filled the old mines around Las Vegas.

Then Julia turned to Lott. "You think I'm right about the women being here?"

"I do," Lott said.

And he did. But again that nagging feeling came up that they were missing something and damned if he could figure out what.

"So let's back up and see if we can figure out when they started to plan this escape," Julia said. "Maybe then we can get a hint as to the plan."

"I know exactly when," Lott said. "When Andor and I found that mine fifteen years ago. We must have scared them to death."

"So they have had fifteen years to plan this exactly," Julia said, sounding as dejected as Lott felt.

"All this time to plan disguises," Lott said, "get fake names, stash away more money than I want to think about under those fake names."

Nothing at all Julia could say to that, so she said nothing.

They sat in silence, watching the poor reporter cut to different reporters around town, clearly not getting any kind of information.

All Lott could think about was the victims.

So many victims.

If somehow he and Andor could have broken this case fifteen years ago, it would have saved so many lives.

Suddenly, Lott turned to Julia. "Did anyone say anything about the woman from Montana? Missy Andrews? Has she been found yet?"

Julia shook her head. Then she quickly pulled out her phone and called Annie.

Lott could hear his daughter's distinctive voice come over Julia's phone.

"Any recovery yet of the woman from Montana?" Julia asked.

"I'll have Fleet do a search of police records and get back to you," Annie said and hung up.

Julia clicked off her phone and put it on the coffee table in front of her. "You think I'm wrong about the woman being left and not killed?"

Lott shook his head. "Honestly, I don't think you are wrong."

He didn't like at all what he was thinking.

"But...?" Julia asked.

Lott took a deep breath and looked into the eyes of the woman he had come to love.

"Andor and I made the assumption that us finding the mine fifteen years ago might have stopped the killer or killers. We could never catch any lead or even a hint that they continued."

Julia nodded, her face now pale. "You think these two might just continue on?"

Suddenly Lott understood what had been nagging at him.

"What happens if they took turns?"

CHAPTER TWENTY-FIVE

AUGUST 15TH, 2015
9:45 A.M.
LAS VEGAS

JULIA JUST LOOKED at Lott, the odd question not making any sense at all.

"Took turns?" she asked.

He nodded, clearly not happy. "We know that West took a leave of absence every month for a week."

Julia nodded.

"What if Lynch did the same thing on a different week?"

Julia felt she might just be sick.

In all her years of working as a detective, she had never imagined anything like this even being possible, let alone for this many years in a row.

"If Andor and I spooked Lynch and West fifteen years ago," Lott said, "what happens if they set up their cover identities then and a parallel operation under one of those cover identities? So Lynch could have some fun as well."

"I hope you are wrong," Julia said, grabbing her phone from the coffee table.

"I hope like hell I am as well," Lott said, sitting back to stare at the poor reporter on the screen doing the best she could with no information.

Julia dialed Annie and quickly put the phone on speaker.

Annie picked up the phone and said simply, "The woman from Montana has not yet been found."

Julia glanced at Lott, who was nodding that he had heard.

"You father has come up with a horrid theory," Julia said. "And I need you and Doc and Fleet to disprove it."

"Go ahead," Annie said, clearly hesitant.

"Your father thinks that when he and Andor found the mine fifteen years ago, they spooked Lynch and West into setting up a parallel system under fake names. Fake everything. And Lynch went out every two weeks to get a victim just as West did."

"Oh, shit," Annie said.

"Search the region for missing women with different hair color," Lott said. "Maybe Lynch had a crush on another girl on that bus. Clearly West was into black hair and had a crush on one of the two girls with black hair who died on the bus. Lynch might have been into a blonde or redhead or brunette."

"Got it," Annie said.

"Prove me wrong," Lott said. "Please?"

"We're going to do our best," Annie said and clicked off the phone.

Julia put the phone down between them on the couch.

"You don't think you are wrong, do you?" Julia asked, looking at Lott, a man she had grown to love and admire over the last year. He was one of the smartest people she knew when it came to putting together crime pieces.

"I hope I am wrong," Lott said. "But if I am right, where would they hide even more bodies?"

"Everything comes back to old mines," Julia said.

"Or old school busses," Lott said, holding up a second finger. "What happens if Lynch is putting her victims, if there are any, in old school busses?"

"Oh, no," Julia said, her heart racing. She knew instantly Lott might be right. And all she could do was sit there and be silent and hope like hell he was wrong.

After what seemed like an eternity of silence, the phone rang, jarring her from horrid and sick thoughts of women being baked alive in school busses. She nodded to Lott and reached down and hit the speaker button.

"Got us both here," Julia said.

"A fourth friend that ran with Lynch and West and the black-haired girl when they were in school was named Cynthia Peters," Annie said. "She had blonde hair, kept her hair long, and she also died on the bus."

Julia didn't like at all where this was going.

Beside her on the couch, Lott was just shaking his head.

Annie went on. "Fleet dropped everything and did a preliminary search of the western states through all the missing person databases, same as he did before, and again he and his people found almost three hundred missing women that matched that very general description of long blonde hair and age range that have gone missing in the last fifteen years. There were almost none before that."

"Shit," Lott said softly. "Just shit, shit, shit."

Annie ignored him. "We are pulling up records of when Lynch was in town now from her business," Annie said. "And Fleet is going to start a search of more mines in the area."

"Tell him not to bother," Lott said.

"Why?" Annie asked. Then she said, "Hang on, let me put Fleet on speaker."

"No need for more mine searches because I'm betting we need to look for a bus graveyard," Lott said when it was clear that Fleet could hear him as well.

"I agree," Julia said. "It would need to be very isolated, yet not a huge distance from Las Vegas. In the desert and the heat, yet well protected."

She didn't like at all what she was thinking, but now that she knew it was possible, and that many women had gone missing, they had to keep working to disprove it.

"I'll get some satellite images coming to you at once," Fleet said. "And we'll work over them here as well."

"Thanks," Julia said as Annie hung up.

"Can this get any worse?" Lott asked, shaking his head.

Julia didn't know what to say.

Then Lott laughed, but without humor. "You know, I remember Andor and me asking ourselves that very same question fifteen years ago."

CHAPTER TWENTY-SIX

AUGUST 15TH, 2015
11:00 A.M.
LAS VEGAS

LOTT HAD CALLED Andor right after hanging up from Annie and said simply, "Get over here. This has gotten worse. We're downstairs. And don't touch the chicken in the fridge when you come in. Trust me, you won't have the stomach for it."

Then he hung up.

Andor had arrived just as the satellite images arrived from Fleet. Annie had told him that they were digging into where old busses went to be recycled or sold. So far no luck, since it was August and a lot of the school districts' personnel were on vacation.

Each satellite image covered about six square miles of desert and there were hundreds of images, at least.

Lott put the images all on a memory stick and then plugged the stick into his television, hooking up his computer keyboard as well so the big screen worked as a computer screen.

Then he and Julia and Andor all pulled chairs from the poker table over to the big screen so they could get moderately close to it.

"So you want to tell me what the hell we're looking for?" Andor asked, sipping on a bottle of water and patting his neck with a wet towel.

"Bus graveyard," Julia said.

"A what?" Andor asked.

"Your partner here believes Lynch went out every month to get a victim just as West did," Julia said.

"Serious?" Andor asked.

"Over three hundred women with long blonde hair missing since we spooked these two monsters fifteen years ago," Lott said.

"So you think they set up their backup and escape plan then?" Andor asked.

"I'm guessing that's exactly what happened," Lott said, glancing at the white face of his partner.

"So we're looking for a bus graveyard in the desert," Julia said, "well-protected and more than likely hidden from normal view."

"Think the busses will be buried?"

"No," Lott said. He just knew they wouldn't be. Again, these women were recreating in a very sick fashion that bus accident over and over and over. Lynch on the bus side, West on the mine side.

"Before we start into this," Julia said, "Any news from headquarters?"

Andor shook his head. "Nothing but the fact that none of the jerky in any of the Lynch shops was made of human flesh."

That jarred Lott. He had expected them to find some, at least behind the counter in some special reserve.

"So where did all that human flesh go?" Julia asked.

Lott just shook his head. "We're missing something there as well."

"We're missing an entire case," Andor said. "We got bodies, but not one lick of evidence. Nothing, and that's driving the chief and the fine people from the FBI nuts."

"Nothing?" Julia said.

"Nothing," Andor said, clearly angry. "Even if we caught these two women, they couldn't be charged with anything. They own mines. So what? West takes a vacation every month? So what? The murders pattern some tragic deaths in their own pasts. So what? No evidence, not a lick of proof so far."

"Is the chief even going to mention them as persons of interest?" Julia asked.

"And get sued from here to Canada and back?" Andor asked. "Their lawyers are already fighting every search warrant. So not a chance."

Lott agreed completely. He had hoped that the human jerky would be the real link. Maybe fifteen years ago, it might have been. But fifteen years ago, he and Lott put these two monsters on notice that they might get caught and the monsters learned.

"So we find their mistake," Lott said, pointing to the screen.

They all turned to stare at the image of the Nevada desert taken from a satellite shot far overhead. The date on the image said it was taken five days before. Newer than Lott would have expected.

On the big screen, they could see almost each individual sagebrush. A large faded-yellow school bus was going to jump off the image like a bad pimple on clear skin.

Lott quickly got them through forty of the images when they found it. Sixty or more school busses filled a corner of the image, most faded to almost white, many parked within feet of each other in rows. A single dirt road led into the compound that was surrounded by what looked like a very high fence.

Julia grabbed the phone and called Annie as Lott leaned in closer, studying the area around the busses. It appeared to be in a shallow rock valley with walls on three sides. It would be impossible to see from any distance at all.

"We found it," Julia said, putting the phone on speaker again so Lott and Andor could hear.

Julia quickly gave the picture image number.

"Tell Fleet to tread lightly with the computer searches on this property," Lott said. "Expect the two killers to have high level warning systems on any search of this property."

"Good thinking, Dad," Annie said. Then, from the sounds of it, she turned slightly away from the phone. "Did you get that, Fleet?"

"Got it," Fleet said from the background. "They will never know anyone looked, I promise. Give me just one minute, so hold on."

Lott went back to studying the images of the busses, wishing he could fly in low like Google images did and see what was in those busses. He had a hunch he would see it much closer soon enough.

"Wampler Recyling Inc. owns the property," Fleet said.

Lott snapped around and looked at Julia, whose eyes were wide.

"Careful, real careful," Lott said. "But can you get us images of Wampler?"

"Why is that name ringing a bell?" Annie asked.

"Kirk Wampler was the kid who survived the bus tragedy and then was killed by a bus," Julia said.

"These two sickos sure have a sense of irony," Andor said.

"Oh, shit," Annie said.

"We are being very careful," Fleet said. "My people have gone to what we call Def-Con Five, meaning any hint of a search could explode everything."

Lott shook his head. There would be no way in hell they could solve some of these cases without Doc and Fleet and Annie and all the power they wielded with their vast money and expert teams.

"You were right," Fleet said. "My team is telling me that very sophisticated search alarms were set on this site. We triggered none of them."

"Good work," Julia said.

Lott made himself take a deep breath.

"Kirk Wampler is the founder of the company," Fleet said after a moment. "It was started in 2001 and has a dozen business locations around the area specializing in metal repurposing and recycling. I am sending an image of Kirk Wampler to all three of you now."

Julia quickly took her iPad and clicked it on, then got her e-mail, opening the image.

The image was of Lynch, hair very short, large fake eyebrows, wearing a three-piece suit. She disguised perfectly as a man.

"Let me guess," Lott said. "Wampler is married."

"In 2001," Fleet said, "to Cynthia Peters. Picture on the way."

Lott didn't need to see the picture. He had no doubt it would be West.

CHAPTER TWENTY-SEVEN

JULIA SAT STARING at the image of the bus graveyard on the screen. She didn't want to even try to imagine what the inside of fourteen or so of those busses would be like. She had no intention of going and looking. She needed to sleep again at some point and her imagination was already enough to keep her awake for more nights than she wanted to think about.

She turned to Lott and Andor, who both seemed to be lost in thought. Andor was just staring at his feet and Lott was doing the same thing she had been doing, just staring at the image of the bus graveyard.

"We need some chicken," she said, standing and turning for the stairs, her phone and iPad in her hand. "And then we need to figure out proof to stop these killers before that woman from Montana becomes the first victim sitting against the wall in another mine."

She headed up the stairs taking them two at a time to try to get some blood flowing back to her shocked brain.

She was putting out paper plates and napkins when both Lott and Andor joined her. Lott had her iced tea glass in his hand and refilled hers and his as Andor pulled out the new bucket of chicken and grabbed himself another bottle of water.

The smell of the chicken filled the kitchen almost instantly. No one said a word until they were all seated and had taken a few bites of the still slightly-warm chicken. To Julia, the taste overcame her desire to never eat again, and actually calmed her some. She figured that was because KFC was part of her normal life, not this insane case.

After another bite, she pulled a spiral notebook from the counter behind her and opened it to a clean page. It was a notebook Lott used for groceries and other items he needed to pick up around town.

"So we are going to make a list," she said. "Of all the things we don't yet know."

"I'd suggest you write the word 'everything' and be done with it," Andor said, wiping chicken grease off his fingers. "But I don't suppose that would help much."

Julia ignored him and said, "Montana woman. Missy Andrews. She's still more than likely alive and out there."

"We can hope," Andor said.

She wrote "Montana Woman" as #1 on the list and circled it.

"Where were all these women baked?" Lott asked.

She wrote that down.

"Why take the meat?" Andor asked.

She wrote that down as well.

"Can we trace the school clothes and where they were bought?" Lott asked. "A lot of years of buying clothes."

Julia doubted that would be possible, but she wrote it down anyway. But it caused her to think of something else as Lott and Andor sat staring at their chicken.

"They are using two names now from the bus tragedy," Julia said. "Are they using others?"

"Oh, shit!" Andor said, standing and moving to where they had left the folder with the information and names from the bus tragedy.

Julia grabbed the phone and called Annie, who answered almost at once.

"You have the file on the bus tragedy and the victims?" Julia asked.

Across the table, Andor was flipping through the old file and Lott was staring at her, nodding.

"We got them all," Annie said.

"We're betting Lynch and West are using all the names in one way or another that were associated with that bus tragedy, including the teacher," Julia said. "Can you have Fleet and his people do the super-careful searches on all the names?"

"Damn, great idea," Annie said. "We should have thought of that. Back with you shortly." She hung up.

Julia put the phone down beside the list, trying to decide if she wanted to try to eat another piece of chicken.

Lott was nodding. "Really good idea."

"I have an even sicker idea," Andor said.

Julia wasn't sure she could imagine a sicker idea in this case.

Andor had taken the file folder from the case 15 years ago and was looking at an autopsy photograph of one of the women.

Julia caught a glance at the picture and instantly looked away. Nothing about a baked and carved up human body that was appealing.

Andor looked up from the file at both of them and closed the folder over the autopsy photographs. He seemed to have a haunted look in his eyes. Julia had never seen Andor look that way before.

He then pointed to the folder of the bus tragedy victims.

"I think we need to quietly dig up a few of these graves," he said.

Julia just stared at Andor, as did Lott. For the life of her she couldn't imagine why they would need to do that, or what it would help.

Finally Lott asked bluntly, "And why would we do that?"

"When I asked about why they take the meat," Andor said, "it dinged me. We have always assumed they took it for eating, standing jokes around headquarters and all. But what happens if that assumption has been flat wrong for all these years."

"What else are you thinking they would take it for?" Julia asked, just about as puzzled as she had been in a long time.

"They take the women's butts, top back of their legs, and underwear," Andor said, pointing to the autopsy file.

Lott and Julia both nodded.

Then she understood where Andor was going.

Silence filled the kitchen like a heavy weight. All Julia could do was blink as she imagined a woman's butt, legs, and underwear mounted on some sort of surface. And over a hundred of them stretching off into the distance.

Nightmare didn't begin to describe that image.

The chicken she had eaten now threatened to make a second showing.

Lott shoved his plate away and stood, clearly angry. He paced over to the counter, then came back.

Julia didn't look up at him. She was afraid to. It was everything she could do to clear the image and keep her lunch down.

"You thinking they went back and got trophies from their first kills?" Lott asked Andor.

Andor nodded.

Lott again paced over to the counter and then came back.

"When you bake a human like that," Lott said, "As I discovered with my long bake of a roast, the flesh becomes easier to cut precisely with very sharp knives."

"Exactly," Andor said. "They could then add moisture back into the skin and then coat it with an epoxy or something else like is done with those parts of human bodies in museums."

Lott nodded. "We have seen sicker trophies taken by killers."

Julia had as well, but not on this scale.

"Looks like both women have a thing for women's butts," Andor said, shaking his head.

"Not both women," Julia said, trying her best to not imagine what they might find in those busses. "We haven't seen the busses. We don't know which part Lynch is cutting off to use as a trophy."

Again the silence just slammed into the kitchen like a hammer, pounding at a headache that was threatening Julia. She forced herself to take long, deep breaths and move her shoulders around and the headache faded back a little. She doubted it would leave until this was all over.

Finally, Lott said, "you are right, we need to dig up a few graves."

At that moment the phone rang.

"It's Annie," Julia said, picking up her phone. "Let's hope we don't have to, because now, if we find their trophy room, we can stop these two cold. We will have the evidence."

CHAPTER TWENTY-EIGHT

LOTT LISTENED OVER the speakerphone and was stunned when Annie and Fleet told them that not only were a few of the names from the bus tragedy being used, but that all of them were active. Including the teacher's name.

"At first glance," Fleet said, "the names all have property and accounts and cash in six western states. All of it started a couple of years after Kirk died."

Fleet paused, then added: "We are digging carefully to not set off any alarms and will be back with you with results in an hour."

"Can you also check in those accounts if one of them bought a lot of clear epoxy-like material," Lott had said.

"The stuff used to seal human flesh like in the museum shows of exposed human skin and muscles," Andor said.

"Something you haven't told us yet?" Annie asked.

"Just see if you can find any reference to that," Lott said, not really wanting to explain any more to his daughter at this point. "Or any kind of taxidermy products that could be used to preserve human muscle and skin."

"Oh, shit," Annie said. "You are kidding."

"A theory is all," Julia said.

"I may never eat again," Fleet said.

Annie hung up.

"So we have another thing to add to our list," Julia said. "Where would they display that many trophies?"

Lott watched as she added that to their list of questions. Then she looked up. "What other details are we missing? Let's start with the bus crash because it seems everything else does."

"Did these two have other friends in school at the time of the accident?" Andor asked.

Lott nodded. Good question and he watched as Julia wrote it down.

They sat there for a short time in silence, thinking. Then Lott realized the one large thing they were missing.

"The school itself," Lott said. "Is it still in operation and if not, who owns it now?"

"Great question," Julia said, and wrote that down as well.

"How about we take a drive past it," Andor said. "I got the address and I need to move around some to let this chicken find a place a little lower than my throat."

Lott could only agree to that.

He grabbed all three of them fresh bottles of water as Julia put the tub of chicken back into the fridge and tossed the paper plates into the garbage.

Andor took a dishtowel, soaked it in cold water, and put it over his neck. Then they headed out the back door and into the afternoon August heat.

It was like stepping into a blast furnace, but at the moment, just the change felt good as far as Lott was concerned. It cleared his mind.

He climbed into his Cadillac SUV and got it started, letting the air-conditioning run at full blast.

Andor got into the back seat and Julia climbed into the passenger seat. She had her phone and his grocery notebook. After this, Lott had no doubt he was going to need a new notebook.

Lott worked his way through traffic out the old Boulder Highway. The ten-minute drive was done in silence. They all needed a change of scenery more than anything else at this point.

From the backseat, Andor said, "Turn right off the highway up here. Three blocks down. If these two killers own this place as well, they will have it monitored, so stay back and don't stop."

"Good thinking," Lott said. He had no doubt that if the school was involved, they would have it monitored.

The neighborhood had long ago seen better days. Most of the homes were built in the 1960s and many of them looked like they hadn't had a coat of paint since they were built. Standard trash neighborhood with junked cars in front yards and no hint at all of landscaping besides rows of tires melting in the sun.

"Go right! Quick," Julia shouted.

Without question, Lott swung the big white SUV down the street to the right. He had just caught a glimpse of the old school ahead of them. It was surrounded by two layers of tall fence with many "No Trespassing" signs. From what he could see, it looked like it had once been under construction, but that had long ago stopped.

The school must have been something nice back in the 1950s. Brick, with tall windows and a wide porch out front. It seemed to be two stories tall and had a bell tower of some sort. No wonder someone had wanted to fix it up at one point.

He had no idea what Julia had seen, but there had been something that had alerted her.

"Why right?" Andor asked just a second before Lott did.

"Stop here, on the side of the street," Julia said. "See the home beside the old school."

Lott nodded. From where they were parked in front of a patch of dirt and weeds, he could barely see the home she mentioned. It looked slightly more kept up than many in this area.

"I am sure I saw Kirk Wampler, otherwise known as Lynch, get in that dark sedan beside the house. And West got in the passenger seat."

"Oh, shit," Andor said.

At that point, the sedan backed out of the driveway slowly, then turned away from them and vanished along the street that ran in front of the old school and parallel to the one they were on.

Julia was instantly on the phone.

Damn Lott hoped she was right. If so, this would be the first piece of luck they had had in this case in fifteen years.

It was about damn time they had some luck.

Lott swung the big SUV around and headed parallel along the street they had seen the sedan go down. He knew that both of these streets dead-ended in a few blocks into a freeway, so the sedan would have to turn toward them to get to the Old Boulder Highway.

After a block, Lott pulled over in front of one of the only houses in the neighborhood that looked kept up. He didn't want them to see him moving.

Just as he did, the sedan went past in front of them, headed for the highway.

Lott eased back into the street.

"Annie, we have an emergency," Julia said, making sure the phone was on speaker. "I think I just saw Lynch and West."

"They are stopped," Lott said, "waiting to turn toward town on the Old Boulder Highway two blocks away from us."

"They are in a dark, late model Chevy sedan," Andor said. "Four-door, can't spot the license plate."

"Can you track them in case we lose them?"

"Fleet?" Annie shouted away from the phone.

"Already on it," Fleet shouted back from what must have been across the office.

Lott just shook his head. Again, no chance they could solve any of this without Doc and Annie and Fleet doing their computer magic.

The sedan turned onto the highway in traffic and headed into town.

Lott got to the intersection and then into traffic quickly, making one car brake suddenly, but at least he was only a dozen cars behind the sedan.

"Can you track us with my phone's location?" Julia asked. "The sedan is only a dozen cars ahead of us in the same lane."

"I got them," Fleet said. "Two people in the car. I'm following them on traffic cams, so you can back off."

Lott let himself take a deep breath and move over a lane.

The sedan made it through a stoplight while they got held up, but Fleet told them not to worry.

After a mile or so of silence, Fleet said, "The car is registered to Kirk Wampler. You hit it on the head. And I know exactly where they are going."

"You're kidding," Julia asked.

"We just got into one of their bank accounts," Fleet said. "Don't ask how. But twice a week they go for a late lunch at the Golden Nugget Buffet. They haven't missed in years."

"So murderers have date nights," Andor said.

"So you can follow them?" Lott asked.

"Without an issue," Fleet said. "Doc and Annie are already out the door headed to the Golden Nugget to alert the security there and let me get plugged into the casino security systems and cameras."

"Don't let them know they are being watched," Lott said.

"No one will get close to them," Fleet said, "and we will make sure any signal trying to reach them from any of their alarms will be shut down completely while they are in there."

"Good," Lott said, "because we're going back to the school."

"School?" Fleet asked.

"The Saint Mary's Girl's School where all this started," Lott said, getting the big white Cadillac turned off the highway and then around and on the highway headed back to the school. "They came from a home beside the old school. I'm betting there is a reason for that."

"We'll keep you on the line," Julia said to Fleet.

They didn't have a lot of time. But they had some.

And Lott had a hunch that the woman from Montana didn't have much time left at all.

PART FIVE

———

CALLING DEAD

CHAPTER TWENTY-NINE

JULIA HAD BEEN stunned for a moment when she saw Lynch dressed as Wampler come out of that home and get into the sedan. Luckily she reacted as fast as she did. Lott's Cadillac was certainly not a car normally seen in this neighborhood, so they would have stuck out and been spotted.

Andor leaned forward between the two front bucket seats as Lott managed to get them headed back toward the school.

"You thinking what I'm thinking?" Andor asked. "Missy Andrews from Montana is being baked as we speak?"

"I am," Lott said.

"Shit," Fleet said over the phone that Julia held up between the three of them.

Julia just shook her head. If that was the case, the woman might already be dead. Or nearly dead.

"I'll get us an emergency search warrant," Andor said. "We play this by the book if we can."

"Agreed," Lott said. "But we go in warrant or not."

Andor nodded and was on the phone a moment later. He simply said his name, then asked for the chief, and less than ten seconds later was connected with the chief. Julia was impressed, considering the firestorm that must be going on at headquarters.

"Chief," Andor said, "We have Lynch and West under surveillance and we think the Montana woman is in immediate danger. We need an emergency warrant. Fast as you can get it."

Julia watched as Lott got parked in front of the old school and Andor gave the address to the chief.

"Fleet," Lott said, "we need to know the instant Lynch and West are blocked from any reception of an alarm."

"A moment," Fleet said.

Julia forced herself to take a deep breath and try to stay calm as each second ticked away in silence.

The old brick school clearly had been special in its day, but now, with two layers of ten-foot tall wire fence around it and construction half done on a bunch of stuff, the school looked just tired. More like an old prison building than anything else. The tall windows had long since been boarded up and the front door was also boarded over.

Julia was surprised that it wasn't bigger. It didn't look much larger than the size of a regular church. But it was two stories tall and the brick bell tower was a bell tower, not a steeple. From what she could tell, the bell was long gone.

"My people just found that Lynch and West," Fleet said on speaker on her phone, "under the Wampler name, own the old school as well, under another shell company that was buried damn deep. And they own three of the homes around the old school."

"Where are they now?" Julia asked. "We're about to go into the school and we don't want to alert them."

"You are clear," Fleet said. "They are just pulling into the valet parking at the Rush Tower side of the Golden Nugget. They are shut down for any incoming messages. Annie and Doc have me linked into all the casino's security cameras and they are standing by in security as well."

"Completely?" Julia asked.

"Completely," Fleet said. "No one in the casino area is going to get a phone call on a cell phone while those two are in there."

Julia glanced at Lott who nodded. "Let's go."

She nodded. They now could go into the school without setting off alarms that would send Lynch and West fleeing.

"We'll let you know what we find in just a few minutes, Chief," Andor said from behind her. "Stay tuned and stall that press conference just a few more minutes."

He clicked off his phone. "Got the warrant."

All three of them climbed out into the baking heat.

Julia kept her connection to Fleet on and held her phone out in front of her as Lott and Andor opened the back of the SUV and dug out a couple large pair of wire and bolt cutters and two large crowbars.

Then they started right at the front gate on the fence.

Two minutes of work in the heat and with the hot wire fence and they had the first gate open enough for the three of them to get inside the area between the two fences. It took less than a minute to get the second fence gate open.

Both Lott and Andor were sweating. But Julia knew that if Missy Andrews was inside, time was of the essence.

"Lynch and West just reached the lobby of the buffet," Fleet said.

"Got a floor plan of this old school?" Lott asked.

"I will pull one up and walk you through it," Fleet said. "Door on the east side might be your best bet to get in."

Julia glanced around as both Fleet and Lott shook their heads. "We're going through the front."

Julia watched, holding the phone out in front of her, wishing there was something she could do as the two of them started ripping boards down. It took them less time to expose the old front door than it had to get through the fence.

"Door's rotted," Lott said, staring up at the casing.

Julia could see that as well.

"Let's hope there's nothing solid behind this," Andor said.

Then with a solid kick, the door smashed inward and came away from the frame, twisting into a wall and sending a cloud of dust swirling through the air.

"Watch for nails," Lott said as they three of them went over the debris and inside.

The place smelled musty and old and unused. A wide main hallway led away in front of them, covered in dust and broken trim and doors, illuminated by the bright light from the broken front door only. On the inside, the place looked much bigger than it did from the outside.

Both Andor and Lott had grabbed flashlights and both started carefully down the hallway.

"Fleet," Julia asked, flipping an old light switch without any success. "Is this place pulling any power?"

"Hold on," Fleet said.

They had taken another five steps down the old high-ceilinged hallway before Fleet came back. "It is. Massive amounts, actually. That started ten minutes ago."

"Oven," Julia said. "Damn it!"

"Basement," Lott said.

"Fleet, is there a basement?" Julia asked.

"There is," Fleet said. "Staircase on the right as you come in from the main door. There is an old gym and locker rooms down there."

Andor cut the lock on the old door with his bolt cutters and they went down the old stairs quickly, plunging into darkness that even the two flashlights didn't seem to push back much.

"Still with us, Fleet?" Julia asked.

"Loud and clear," Fleet said.

At the bottom of the stairs there were two doors, both of which looked like they had been used a great deal. Both had high-level security locks on them. Keypad electronic types.

"That door looks like it goes off underground toward the home next door," Lott said.

Julia agreed. "A logical way to get unseen into the old school."

"Let's hope they didn't set any kind of explosive trap on this door," Lott said.

"Too damn late now if they did," Andor said.

Julia agreed as both Lott and Andor started banging at the door, smashing anything that would smash.

"That's some noise," Fleet said.

"Breaking into the old gym area, from the looks of it," Annie shouted over the destruction.

Finally, the door frame started to move where it had rotted out along one side. And then a moment later, it fell inward with a smash, sending dust swirling into the big room.

Cool air swept over them as they stepped forward.

A switch on the wall beside the ruined door worked this time as Julia tried it and lights in the old gym came up full and bright.

At first she didn't understand what she was seeing exactly.

Then the details came clear and she covered her mouth and turned away and for the first time in all her years as a detective, she threw up.

And right beside her, Lott did the same thing.

On the phone in Julia's hand, Fleet said softly, "That doesn't sound good."

CHAPTER THIRTY

LOTT HAD NEVER, not once, lost his lunch over a crime scene. But what faced them in this room was so much more than a crime scene. This was a sick trophy room.

And just the vastness of the death had overwhelmed him.

He managed to clear his mouth by spitting a few times, then eased Julia up from where she was bent over and together they both turned around again.

The scene in front of them was a nightmare that he had no doubt he would ever forget.

On what looked like very narrow twin beds, with sheets, women's butts, partially covered with underwear, and the backs of their legs were posed, two per bed. It looked like the rest of the woman's body was simply covered up under the sheet, so it looked very much like women were laying there, face down, side-by-side on the narrow beds.

That would have been bad enough, but it didn't stop there.

Between each bed were two child mannequins dressed in the black and white schoolgirl uniforms, standing posed as if watching the two partial bodies on the beds. One watched one bed, another watched another bed.

Only each child mannequin had a real woman's head with long blonde hair.

The bus graveyard was going to be full of headless women's bodies. Lynch took their heads as a trophy.

The scene was repeated like a giant dormitory all the way around the outside of the large gym and also had started another row down the middle.

Sick trophies from over three hundred dead women.

"We need to find that oven," Andor said, his breathing heavy, his voice raspy.

"Damn," Julia said, shaking her head.

Lott also snapped back into focusing on what was important. It was as if his mind had just gone from him for a moment and now it was suddenly back. He forced himself to not look into the faces of all the women whose heads were posed on the child mannequin bodies.

A door stood partially open on the other side of the gym and Andor pointed to it.

Lott, with Julia at his side, followed Andor toward the door as fast as they could go, not looking at anything on or beside any of the beds.

"You still with us?" Julia said into the phone she carried.

"Right with you," Fleet said. "All three of us are here on the phone if you need anything at all."

Lott was glad to hear that, but his strongest hope at the moment was that his daughter would never see anything like this.

Once through the door, Julia again flicked on the light and there, in front of them, was what looked like a massive pizza oven.

And it was radiating heat.

Andor moved to the control panel to the right of the big door and shut everything down quickly. Then with a glance at Lott and Julia, he opened the door.

Heat, as if they had stepped back outside into the hot August sun, flooded the small room.

Inside the oven, stretched out nude, was a black-haired woman lying on what looked to be a very thick pad of some sort.

Lott had not seen a picture of Missy Andrews, but he was betting that was her.

He grabbed an oven mitt and tossed a second one to Andor, then the two of them rolled the large tray the woman was on out of the oven. Lott wasn't surprised that it came easily.

Julia quickly touched the woman's hot skin searching for a pulse.

"She's still alive. And her heartbeat is strong."

Lott couldn't believe the relief he felt at that instant.

"Fleet," Julia said into her phone. "Get an ambulance headed here at once."

"On the way," Fleet said.

Andor had his phone to his ear as well. "Chief, I need just you, the head of the FBI, and the State Police person in charge to come here at once. Don't let reporters follow you."

Andor listened for a moment. "Postpone it for an hour and then you can announce you have wrapped this all up."

A pause.

"Not kidding," Andor said.

Another pause as Andor listened. Then he said simply, "We found their trophy room and the Montana woman is alive."

"Make it fast," Andor said. Then hung up.

Lott just shook his head, then pointed to the woman on the big oven tray. "We have to get her upstairs and out of here."

Julia nodded. "We can't have some poor ambulance drivers seeing that room out there."

"Agreed," Andor said. "No one deserves to live with that image."

Lott looked around and spotted the ambulance-like gurney tucked to one side of the oven. More than likely Lynch and West had used it to bring their victims in. It was set at the same height as the oven tray.

Lott grabbed the gurney and pulled it so that it was in front of the oven. With Julia keeping the gurney from moving, Lott and Andor lifted the woman, pad and all, onto the gurney.

Then Julia used a light sheet from a table nearby to cover her up a little.

"Back through the nightmare," Andor said.

Lott nodded.

He knew he was going to be living this nightmare for a very long time.

CHAPTER THIRTY-ONE

JULIA LED THE way back through the gym, focusing on making sure the gurney they were pushing didn't hit anything. The last thing she wanted to do was stop and look at the heads of murder victims and all the parts of bodies from other women.

At the ruined door, Lott and Andor managed to get the gurney over the wood on the floor and to the bottom of the old staircase. It was markedly warmer out in the foyer area, and Julia didn't much like taking a woman clearly overheated out into the Vegas sun and heat, but they had no choice.

Lott lifted one end of the gurney and then put it back down. "We should be able to get this up the stairs if we are careful."

"I'll pull from the top," Julia said.

Andor nodded and he and Lott got around behind the gurney as Julia got up a few stairs.

"Fleet," she said into her phone, "I'm keeping the connection, but putting the phone in my pocket while we try to get this poor woman up these stairs."

"Understood," Fleet said. "Lynch and West just got their first salad course."

Julia put the phone in her front pocket as Andor and Lott nudged the gurney up against the bottom of the old staircase.

"Count of three," Lott said.

"Three," Andor said.

Andor and Lott lifted while Julia pulled up and lifted. Surprisingly the gurney went up the step easily.

"Three," Andor said again.

Another step.

They repeated that as fast as they dared, with Andor and Lott almost holding one end of the gurney up at chest level.

Finally, they had the poor woman and the hospital gurney in the main hallway. They wheeled it quickly toward the front door just as sirens were sounding outside.

They stopped just inside the front door. Lott and Andor were both sweating and breathing hard, but looked as if they would be all right if they got into some cool air and a bottle of water or two.

Julia again checked to see how the woman was doing. Her heart rate was still strong.

"Still doing fine," Julia said.

Lott, breathing hard, and sweating, looked at Julia and nodded and smiled.

Julia was breathing as hard as he was, and she had no doubt her light blouse was stained through sweat and dirty from all the dust. But at this moment, she didn't care. They had managed to rescue this poor woman from two of the worst serial killers in modern times.

And stopping any more killing.

And that was all that mattered.

She pulled the phone from her pocket as Andor went out through the smashed front door and waved as the ambulance pulled up.

"Fleet," Julia asked, taking the phone from her pocket. "You still there?"

"I am," Fleet said. "Are you three all right?"

"We needed a workout today," Lott said.

"And the woman?"

"Still alive," Julia said.

"Great job," Annie said.

"Oh, thank heavens," Fleet said.

Julia could not have agreed more. They had gotten very lucky to be here in time.

Barely in time.

From just outside the front door, Andor turned back to Lott and Julia. "Chief just pulled up as well."

"We give him a ten minute explanation of the bus graveyard and everything Fleet and his people have found," Lott said. "Fleet, you all right with that?"

"I'll put it in a presentable package as supposition and suggestions," Fleet said, "they can research it themselves then so it can go in as evidence."

"Perfect," Lott said.

"So after we tell them everything, what next?" Julia asked.

"We let the chief and his friends go downstairs and lose their lunches," Lott said. "We have a couple at the Golden Nugget I want to join for a late lunch."

"Oh, I'm going to look forward to watching that," Fleet said.

Julia was as well.

At that moment, two men dressed in medical uniforms came in and immediately started working on Missy Andrews.

"She was exposed to high heat and is drugged," Julia said. "So extreme heat stroke measures are in order."

Julia then gave the ambulance men Missy's name and that the police would be contacting her and her family shortly. That she needed to stay away from any press until the police talked with her when she recovered.

Both men nodded.

The chief and two other men in suits picked their way through the rubble as the two from the ambulance changed the woman over to their gurney and headed out into the heat, covering her with a light sheet held up and off her body.

Julia pushed the gurney they had gotten from downstairs off to one side.

"Great job saving her," the chief said, staring after the two ambulance drivers.

"Please keep us out of it," Andor said.

Lott and Julia nodded, and the other two looked puzzled.

Julia didn't do this for credit and she knew that Andor and Lott wanted none either.

The chief turned to the medium-sized man with the blue tie and no hair. "FBI Regional Director Steve Couch."

The man nodded.

"And this is Chief Carl Landers with the State Police," Chief Beason said, indicating a tall, skinny man with hard, dark eyes.

"This is Detectives Lott, Williams, and Rogers," Chief Beason said, finishing the introduction.

Julia noticed that he didn't add the word "retired" to the introduction, which was good because at the moment she felt a long ways from retired.

"Here's what we got, Chief," Andor said. "This morning we started down the idea that Lynch killed just as West did. We discovered that the girl she had a crush on that died in the bus tragedy was named Cynthia Peters. She had long blonde hair at the time."

"West has long blonde hair," the chief said.

All three nodded.

"So we had Doc and Fleet's people do a search for missing women with long blonde hair," Lott said.

"Fleet," Julia said, holding up the phone so that everyone could see it and hear Fleet clearly, "tell them what you found on that search."

"Chief," Fleet said, "We found in a first-pass search the same pattern as the black-haired women. It seems that over the last fifteen years almost two hundred blonde-haired women have gone missing in the western states."

"Oh, shit," FBI Director Couch said.

Julia was glad that Andor pushed on at that point.

"We figured," Andor said, "that if West was hiding the bodies in mines, Lynch had to be hiding the bodies she took in another way."

Before the chief could ask a question, Lott kept the story going. "We then figured out that all the names of the kids in the original bus tragedy were all being used."

"And we had the idea to look for bus graveyards," Julia said, "since that tragedy happened in a bus and these two seemed to be duplicating so much from that tragedy."

The chief and the other two men just nodded. All three of them were sweating in the heat of the hallway. The chief had pulled off his suit jacket and had it over his shoulder.

"We found a bus graveyard," Andor said, "owned by Wampler Industries, heavily protected outside of the city in a hidden valley."

"We didn't go near it because we knew, just as with the mines, it would be watched," Julia said.

"Wampler?" the chief asked.

"Kirk Wampler was the son of the bus driver in the original tragedy," Lott said. "He was the only one who survived and then supposedly committed suicide by stepping in front of a school bus."

"Under a shell company," Fleet said, from the phone, "the old school and some of the homes around the school are owned by Wampler and his wife, Cynthia Peters."

The chief nodded. "Let me guess. Cynthia Peters is West, Wampler is Lynch pretending to be a guy."

"Exactly," Andor said. "Next we worked on why there was no human jerky out there. It seems that assumption we all made fifteen years ago was wrong. They didn't take the body parts as food, they took them as a trophy."

"A woman's butt, underwear, and back of her legs?" Director Couch asked.

"Cut off after baking," Lott said, "then brought back and preserved like they do the skin and muscles in those museum shows on human bodies."

"Oh, shit," Couch said again.

"You found that woman in the oven baking, didn't you?" the chief asked.

Andor nodded.

The chief just shook his head. "Thank heavens you three and Doc and Annie and Fleet and his people never seem to rest."

No one said anything to that, but Julia was glad the chief noticed at least, especially the incredible work that Doc and Annie and Fleet were doing.

"So did Lynch and West leave evidence this time?" FBI Director Couch asked.

"I think in this old school," Julia said, "and that home connected by a tunnel next door, you are going to find all the evidence you will ever need on these two."

Both Lott and Andor nodded to that.

"You said you had them wrapped up?" FBI Director Couch asked.

Julia was starting to like the bald guy. He was direct and seemed to keep on focus.

"We do," Andor said. "They don't know it yet and Lott and I want to pay them a short visit first before you take them."

The chief looked puzzled.

"We have been living with this nightmare for fifteen years," Lott said. "Since that first step into that mine. We just ask for a minute. Trust us, we won't hurt the case in any way."

"Besides," Andor said. "All three of you are going to need to be there with some press to record the capture, and we want no part of that. But first, you need to see what those two women did."

Andor pointed to the staircase leading down. "When you have this place secured and are ready for the photo arrests, call me and we'll let you know where we are at. But don't take longer than fifteen minutes."

The chief nodded and the three men started for the stairs.

"Gentlemen," Julia said. "I would suggest you leave your coats and ties on the gurney there."

"That bad?" the chief said, taking off his tie and putting it with his coat.

"Your worst nightmare," Andor said. "But you all need to see it to understand everything about this case and what kind of monsters you are dealing with."

With that, Julia led the way out the shadows of the hallway and through the front door of the old girls school, picking her way through the rubble to finally be in the hot, blazing sun of a Las Vegas afternoon.

It felt wonderful.

CHAPTER THIRTY-TWO

LOTT GOT THE air-conditioning blowing hard and the Cadillac headed toward town on the Old Boulder Highway. It felt great to just have that much be normal for a moment.

None of them said a word as he drove, being careful.

Finally, after a few minutes, Fleet spoke from the phone Julia still held in her hand.

"Update on the Missy Andrews' condition," Fleet said. "She's going to make a full recovery and she has some relatives who are local who are headed to the hospital now."

"Wonderful," Lott said.

Julia beamed at him and he smiled back. That felt flat out wonderful.

They hadn't been able to save all the other lives, but one was enough for the day. And now they were going to stop any more killing from happening.

"Thanks, Fleet," Lott said. "For everything. We wouldn't have saved her without you."

Nothing from the other side of the phone this time.

"So how are the two monsters?" Andor asked.

"Just finishing their main course," Fleet said. "Doc and Annie are sitting about five tables away. Casino security has the entire place secured down."

"Have them keep an opening for three right beside Lynch and West."

"Will do," Fleet said. "But something you should know."

"Go ahead," Lott said, suddenly being worried again.

"Security scans show they are both carrying concealed weapons. Small pistols."

Lott glanced at Julia, then back at Andor, who just nodded.

"Thanks, Fleet," Lott said. "We'll keep that in mind."

Ten minutes later, Fleet handed a five-dollar tip to the parking valet at the Golden Nugget Rush Tower entrance and the three of them headed inside.

All three of them stopped at a rest room to splash water on their faces and Lott had never felt anything so wonderful as the handfuls of cold water.

Andor took some wet paper towels and just wiped off the back of his neck. Then they went back out and joined Julia, whose face looked flushed as well from the cold water.

"Our trapped mice are starting into their desserts," Fleet said.

"Thanks, Fleet," Julia said. "I'm leaving the connection, but putting the phone in my pocket again."

"I'll be watching," Fleet said. "But just remember, they are trapped and therefore dangerous."

"Copy that," Lott said.

At that moment, Andor's phone rang. He listened for a moment, then said, "They are in the buffet at the Golden Nugget. I would come in with only you three and cameras and a few arresting officers. We'll sit on them until you get here."

Then he put his phone away and smiled at Lott and Julia. "Seems we are about to wrap this up after fifteen years."

"And close a lot of cases and save a lot of lives," Julia said.

Andor nodded to that and turned and headed for the escalator that led up to the buffet.

Julia took Lott's hand and he squeezed her hand in appreciation. He couldn't imagine going through all this with anyone else. They made an amazing team.

As they walked around the planter that divided the buffet from the lobby area, Lott was surprised at how simply normal the two looked.

Lynch made a decent man in looks, and wore a light blue sports coat that clearly screamed money.

West had her long blonde hair pulled back and had on a light blue blouse with pearls around her neck and pearl earrings.

How could two of the worst serial killers in history look so plain and normal?

Doc and Annie sat two tables over to the left of the killers, with an empty table between them and the killers.

Andor led over to the table on the other side of the two killers and sat down.

Julia sat the farthest from the two, while Lott sat across from Andor.

Both of them were close and could move quickly. Lott was almost right beside Lynch.

"Something to drink?" A waitress asked as they were being seated.

"Two glasses of water each," Lott said. "Climbing around inside an old school building is thirsty work."

Both Lynch and West glanced at them, then West did a double-take.

Lott was surprised that she recognized them. He wasn't sure what he thought of that.

"You know," Andor said, "for being dead, Kirk, you are looking pretty nice. A real girly-man if you get my meaning."

"Cynthia here looks much better than she did after being baked on that bus," Lott said. "She has recovered so well."

Both Lynch and West just stared at their half-finished desserts, their hands on the table in front of them. Lynch had been eating apple pie with a slight bit of ice cream. West had been working on a Key lime pie.

Lott didn't much like how they were acting. They had the look of desperation which could mean they would go for their guns at any moment.

Lott glanced at Andor, then at Julia.

Both were clearly seeing the same warning signs.

"You had to assume that someday your killing spree would be over," Andor said, continuing to poke at the two killers. "But I bet you didn't expect two old detectives to be the ones to stop you, now did you?"

"You are right, Detective Williams," West said. "We did expect this to come to an end."

"And you planned for it, right?" Lott said. "All sorts of ways of escape."

"We planned for every contingency," Lynch said, looking at West. "Didn't we, my love."

"We did," West said, nodding.

Lott's alarm bells went off inside his head as he suddenly realized the two of them were planning a mutual suicide, more than likely right here in the casino. And those were their key words to do it.

He jumped at Lynch at the same time as Andor jumped at West.

Lynch's hand was on a gun, and Lott wrestled with her until suddenly Doc and Annie were there as well.

Lott got the gun away and put it on the table where he had been sitting.

Then he made sure Lynch was sitting back in front of her dessert.

Andor and Julia had gotten the gun from West and had done the same thing.

Casino security had materialized all around the buffet, but when Doc waved them away, none of them came in.

"Just stay seated," Lott said to the two killers. "You have some fine folks to meet in a few minutes. Trust me, you do not want to miss this by doing something silly like killing yourselves."

Around them, the buffet was buzzing with noise as both women adjusted where they sat, both looking shocked that their suicide plan had failed so quickly.

Doc and Annie took the two guns and tucked them away and then moved back toward the cashier, but didn't go back to their table.

Lott and Andor sat back down, as did Julia.

Lott glanced at the two killers. "You know why we didn't let you two just save the state a ton of money and kill yourselves?"

Neither woman moved.

"Because there are upwards of three hundred families out there that need closure on the family members you killed," Andor said.

"And we want your two faces to be known as the ugliest killers in modern times," Lott said.

"There will be no escape for either of you," Andor said.

Both women said nothing, simply stared at their hands in front of them.

"Cavalry," Julia said, softly.

Lott glanced around and saw the chief and the director of the FBI coming up the escalator.

Lott and Andor and Julia all stood.

"We needed this little time as well for some closure for us," Lott said.

Andor pointed to the half-eaten desserts. "Might want to finish those. Might be the last dessert either of you see in a very long time."

Then, as Lott turned away, he decided to ask just one question.

"That bus tragedy was horrible," Lott said, stopping over the two women. "But not sure why both of you decided to continue to live it over and over."

West looked up at Lott and just shook her head. "You don't understand yet, do you, detective?"

"It wasn't horrible," Lynch said, looking at Lott with cold, dark eyes. "It was gloriously wonderful."

"Better than we had planned," West said.

"A lot better than we had ever hoped," Lynch said.

"Glorious," West said, softly. "Just glorious."

With that the two women reached forward and took each other's hands.

CHAPTER THIRTY-THREE

THREE WEEKS LATER

SEPTEMBER 3RD, 2015
5:30 P.M.
LAS VEGAS

LOTT UNLOADED THE snacks and drink supplies for the game later while Julia got the bucket of KFC on the kitchen table and then put out a few large piles of napkins and three paper plates.

In theory, Andor was bringing a new cold case for the gang tonight and Lott had made him promise to not make it personal to him or Julia. They hadn't taken on a new case since finally getting rid of Lynch and West.

Both Lynch and West had spent the last three weeks on suicide watch as the national news descended on Las Vegas. A media storm didn't even begin to describe what hit.

The chief had done as he had promised and kept the three of them, plus Doc and Annie and Fleet, out of it all. When asked how the police had come up with all this and solved this very cold case, he had just said simply, "Great detective work."

All the bodies had been removed from the mines and the bus graveyard and all but a few of the victims had been claimed by families.

The national news for a week was full of funerals all over the west as closure finally came for so many.

And the chief had also played up the rescue of Missy Andrews from Montana and her last minute save from an oven. Luckily, Missy made a full recovery and remembered nothing from the moment in the parking lot with a flat tire to when she woke up in the Las Vegas hospital.

Gory details about the two killers had come out, and slowly more and more charges were being placed against them, both in state courts and in federal courts, since kidnapping and murder over state lines were federal crimes.

It seemed like every district attorney with a victim wanted a part of the two killers. It was going to take a lot of time to sort out who got to them first. More than likely the Feds would win, Lott was sure.

Doc and Annie and Fleet had headed back to Idaho after a few days and Doc and Annie had gone in rafting on the River of No Return in central Idaho, where Doc was a guide. They were due out in three more days.

Lott had only had major nightmares a few times during the last few weeks, and Julia had been there for him on both.

She had had her share of bad dreams as well, and he had been there to help her through those. A perfect team to fight nightmares.

But for Lott, it seemed that closing this case, locking up the two killers, cleared out so many of the nightmares that had haunted him for years.

And now, after three weeks, that was feeling very light and free-ing and he was ready to get back to work on another case.

Just as Julia got the plates out and Lott had taken the lid off the tub of KFC to release the fantastic smell of hot chicken into the kitchen, the back door opened and in walked Andor, followed by Chief Beason.

Lott was surprised, but not that surprised. He had come to really like and admire the chief and how he handled all this massive turmoil.

"Wow, does this place smell great," Beason said, smiling.

"Great seeing you, Chief," Julia said as she grabbed him a paper plate and a pile of napkins and pointed to a spot at the table where Annie usually sat.

"Great seeing you as well, Chief," Lott said. "Andor tells me things are finally starting to calm down some."

"Some," Beason said, slipping around to the spot Julia had point-ed to at the table. "I just wanted to come by and thank all three of you personally. And the Cold Poker Gang in general."

Lott smiled. "Thanks," he said.

Julia nodded, as did Andor in agreement.

"But thanks go to you," Lott said, "for giving us the permission to do the job we love and make a difference."

Chief Beason laughed. "I get three of the best detectives I have ever had the pleasure to meet working for me for free and making me and the rest of the clowns down at headquarters look smart. What's not to love on my side?"

"Perfect," Lott said.

"We got a new case," Andor said, pointing to a file he had put on the counter.

"One close to my heart," Chief Beason said, smiling. "So hope you all can pull your magic on that one."

"Oh, great," Lott said, shaking his head, but smiling.

"By the way," Beason said, "I do have one bone to pick with you three from this last case. You could have saved me going into that basement."

Andor laughed and shook his head. "You and Couch and Landers needed to see that to really understand the depth of sickness of those two women."

"And the scale of the tragedy that needed to be dealt with," Julia said.

"Yeah, I know," Beason said. "Just glad no cameras were around to catch the three top law enforcement officers in the area all throwing up together. Felt like a bad night back in college. First time I ever lost my lunch over any crime scene."

"You weren't alone with that one," Lott said.

"So what is your secret?" Beason asked. "Besides being smart and having your daughter and Doc and Fleet helping, how does the Cold Poker Gang solve so many unsolved cases?"

"You honestly want to know?" Andor asked, staring with his look of intensity at the chief.

Lott smiled at Julia.

"I do," the chief said, looking slightly puzzled that his light question was being taken so seriously.

"KFC before every meeting," Andor said, pulling the bucket toward himself and grabbing a wing.

"He's not kidding," Julia said, yanking the bucket to her and grabbing a wing as well.

"He's not," Lott said, grabbing a leg and biting into the juicy, warm meat.

The chief smiled, shook his head, and then pulled the bucket toward himself and grabbed a thigh, biting into it and letting the grease get on his face.

"See what I mean?" Andor asked.

The Las Vegas Chief of Police nodded and smiled. "I do. I feel smarter already."

"Best crime-fighting food ever," Lott said, holding up a half-eaten chicken leg in salute.

They all saluted with their own half-eaten chicken part, and with that the laughter filled the room and the Cold Poker Gang was ready for a new case.

Read the mystery that started the series with the first
Cold Poker Gang novel, *Kill Game,* available now from your
favorite bookseller. Turn the page for a sample chapter.

CHAPTER ONE

MAY, 1992
DOWNTOWN LAS VEGAS, NEVADA

THE IDEA JIM HAD on a warm early-summer evening was to find the rumored place for afterhours dancing called "The Path." Jim had just graduated high school, the proud class of 1992. He was headed next year to Stanford, full academic ride, and he was really looking forward to getting out of the desert in a couple months. He had been born and raised here and was excited about living somewhere else. Anywhere, actually.

Jim stood barely five-nine, had long brown hair, and a moustache he was doing his best to grow and mostly failing.

Sharon, his girlfriend over the last six months, also now graduated, wasn't happy he was going so far away. She had been offered a scholarship at UNLV and had taken it. So between them there was a tension of the coming split.

Sharon was actually taller than Jim, with long blonde hair and skinny legs that seemed to always be stuffed into jeans a size too small. She had also done some light modeling and as she aged, she just got better looking.

Jim had no idea what she saw in him, but they always had such a good time together. They had two hobbies: Dancing and having sex in every place they could imagine or risk.

Tonight they were thinking of doing both at the same time. They had heard how really crowded the dance floor at "The Path" could be. Sharon had suggested, with a smile, that it might be fun to try a little "fooling around" on the floor while dancing.

Jim was game if she was. With Sharon, he would try just about anything. Logic often never played a part.

So they parked down on Paradise Road, about two blocks from the club, and headed down the sidewalk along the row of low warehouses, holding hands and laughing, the coming separation only a distant thing to ignore on such a wonderful spring night.

The club had an entrance off an alley into a large warehouse, but until two days ago, on Sharon's birthday, both of them hadn't been eighteen and old enough to get in, so they hadn't tried to find it.

Paradise had street lights and even though the area felt rough, both of them were native to the city and knew this really wasn't a bad area. They were as safe as they could be at midnight in Las Vegas.

Cars lined the street on both sides, so they knew they were in the right area even though they didn't know exactly where the club was. And between traffic on the street, if they listened hard, they could hear the pounding beat of the music echoing through the one-story buildings of the area.

"Maybe it's down here?" Sharon asked, pulling Jim into the first alley they came to.

Jim could tell at once they were in the wrong place.

And then the smell hit them.

The putrid smell of something rotting in the heat. It was a cloying smell that seemed to make the air thicker than it actually was, and fill every sense. It turned his stomach instantly. He knew it was a dead person instantly. He had smelled that before. He had no idea how police who worked around dead bodies ever got used to the smell.

"What is that?" Sharon asked, stopping and covering her mouth and nose. After a moment she started to back toward the street, her eyes round and her skin pale.

Jim stood his ground. He had been with two friends last year up on Lake Mead when they found a floater near the shore. He knew that smell. Someone had died.

But there was no body in the alley. Just walls of warehouses. Not even garbage cans.

He stepped toward one wall and the smell decreased.

"Jim, get out of there," Sharon said from the sidewalk behind him.

He motioned to her that he would be right there, then stepped toward the other wall. Originally a white stucco wall, it was now stained with years of grime and lack of paint that he could see even in the dark shadows.

And the smell got much worse.

There was no door in the wall, just a nearby high window that was cracked slightly.

Someone was dead in that room beyond that window.

He turned and went back to Sharon, taking her hand. They went around to the front of the building, took down the address, then said, "We have a phone call to make."

He could see a pay phone a block away on the outside wall of a closed grocery store, so he started off in that direction.

"I thought we were going dancing?" Sharon asked, scrambling along in her high heels, working to keep up with his fast strides.

"We are," he said. "But we have to call the police first."

"Why?" she asked.

"That smell," he said.

"You are going to report a smell to the police?" she asked. "It was bad, but not a criminal offense I'm sure."

"I wouldn't be so sure of that," Jim said, letting go of her hand as they reached the phone and he started digging into his pocket for change.

"What do you mean?" Sharon asked, looking worried. There was one thing he really liked about Sharon. She was smart and knew he was smart, so they trusted each other on a lot of things.

"I've smelled that smell before," he said, as he dropped the coin into the phone and pushed zero for operator.

He glanced back at her puzzled expression.

"Near the body I found up at Lake Mead."

She put her hand over her mouth and even in the strange lights of the street, he could see she had lost most of her tan very suddenly.

The operator answered and he was connected to the police. He gave them his name, his location, and the address of the building.

Then he said clearly, "I want to report a dead body."

ABOUT THE AUTHOR

USA Today bestselling author Dean Wesley Smith published more than a hundred novels in thirty years and hundreds and hundreds of short stories across many genres.

He wrote a couple dozen *Star Trek* novels, the only two original *Men in Black* novels, Spider-Man and X-Men novels, plus novels set in gaming and television worlds. He wrote novels under dozens of pen names in the worlds of comic books and movies, including novelizations of a dozen films, from *The Final Fantasy* to *Steel* to *Rundown*.

He now writes his own original fiction under just the one name, Dean Wesley Smith. In addition to his upcoming novel releases, his monthly magazine called *Smith's Monthly* premiered October 1, 2013, filled entirely with his original novels and stories.

Dean also worked as an editor and publisher, first at Pulphouse Publishing, then for *VB Tech Journal*, then for Pocket Books. He now plays a role as an executive editor for the original anthology series *Fiction River*.

For more information about his work, go to www.deanwesleysmith. com, www.smithsmonthly.com or www.fictionriver.com.

Printed in Great Britain
by Amazon

51359346R00121